TELL ME You WANT ME

Love is easy, heartbreak is hard

MADEEHA SUNDUS SHAH

BlueRose ONE
Stories Matter
NewDelhi • London

BLUEROSE PUBLISHERS
India | U.K.

Copyright © Madeeha Sundus Shah 2024

All rights reserved by author. No part of this publication may be reproduced, stored in a retrieval system or transmitted in any form or by any means, electronic, mechanical, photocopying, recording or otherwise, without the prior permission of the author. Although every precaution has been taken to verify the accuracy of the information contained herein, the publisher assume no responsibility for any errors or omissions. No liability is assumed for damages that may result from the use of information contained within.

BlueRose Publishers takes no responsibility for any damages, losses, or liabilities that may arise from the use or misuse of the information, products, or services provided in this publication.

For permissions requests or inquiries regarding this publication, please contact:

BLUEROSE PUBLISHERS
www.BlueRoseONE.com
info@bluerosepublishers.com
+91 8882 898 898
+4407342408967

ISBN: 978-93-6261-491-9

Cover design: Shivam
Typesetting: Namrata Saini

First Edition: April 2024

About the Author

Born in India, Tell Me You Want Me is Madeeha Sundus Shah's first fictional Novel.

"Ever Happier" was her first non-fiction Book which gained her the title of "BEST NON FICTION BOOK" Award 2024 by BlueRose Publications. She has a degree in Journalism and Mass Communication and Counselling Psychology and a certificate in Digital Marketing. She has written few short published stories. She is an Editor of a monthly e-magazine named "Vivid Vision". She is a philanthropist and an avid Reader and Writer.

Contact info- Madishah42@gmail.com
Instagram- that_hijabi_food_blogger
           and
           maddiiwrites

"Let's switch roles, you wait and I won't come back."

-Mahmoud Darwish

Chapter-1

I love winter. I love how coffee and hot chocolate taste much better during the season. I love trying new cafes and new flavors of hot chocolate launched during Thanks giving and Christmas. While hanging out with my friends and trying out cafes, I came across a café that is famous for its beautiful ambience and very friendly waiters. So, me and my friends decided to step in and ask waiters to take our orders. "One hot chocolate for me, please"- I said. The waiter smiled and nodded his head, "sure, mam."

"And what would you like to have, Mam?" The waiter asked my friend Leila with a smile on her face.

"One Shawarma and one Coke for me, please"— being a foodie, Leila replied with full enthusiasm.

Sure, Mam, the waiter smiled again and left.

"I hate waiting for food when I am so hungry" said Leila with full frustration.

Good things take time. I smiled and winked at her face.

I don't know how you can have patience for food, Serah, and I said the same thing again. You need to wait for the good things to come, and she shrugged me off.

See, here came the good things. I told Leila when the waiter brought us our order.

Hot chocolate for you, mam, and a shawarma and a coke for you, said the waiter and left.

"The weather is so cold", I told Leila while sipping my cup of hot chocolate.

"Yes, the best weather for a nice cuppa of hot chocolate" Leila said, nibbling on her shawarma filled with chunks of chicken, mayonnaise, lettuce, onions, and French fries." While enjoying my hot cup and looking at the diverse group of people enjoying their meals, my eyes got stuck on a face, and my heart started pounding as I looked at him again. There was something magical about him—about his face, about his personality—that kept me looking at him again and again. He was sitting four tables away in a black adidas shirt with golden strips on it and black adidas pants, and I kept wondering why I could not look away from this face. Why do I want to get up, go to him and talk? Why does he look so charming to me in a room full of other charming people? I sipped on my hot chocolate and looked across the table again. He was busy having his coffee and talking to his friends and did not notice that I was gazing at him, gazing at his face, so that for once he could look at me and notice my face as well. His charming smile lit up the cold night, and the way he kept moving his hands while talking made him look more beautiful. I felt a sense of connection the minute I saw him. This huge café instantly became my favorite hangout spot. This rooftop café has the best hot chocolate in the city, and it's so full in the winter that you have to wait in line to get your seat. Beautiful golden lights hanging from the beam, colorful small round tables, and colorful chairs made this café a bit different from the mundane cafes of the city. While cold air touching your nose and making your teeth clutter gave the best one hour of your life to make you feel fresh and alive, and a cuppa of hot chocolate worked as a cherry on the cake.

As the night got colder, we left the place to get the cab to our respective homes. I love Scotland. The winters are a bit harsher and colder, but this place is immensely beautiful. I was looking at the sideways trees, which were glittering with Christmas lights, making the whole city bright. I took the cab to my home and told the driver to drive slowly because I wanted to dwell on the meeting with that stranger. I wanted to think about him—about his beautiful, bright face, about his existence, about the minutes and seconds I spent looking at him.

I reached home within 25 minutes because the driver was driving slowly. otherwise, It only takes ten to fifteen minutes from my home to the Chocolab Café.

I removed my shoes at the door and kept them in the shoe rack. I grabbed my night suit and changed into my comfy pajamas.

While in bed, I was thinking about tonight and how his face kept flashing in front of my eyes.

Oh my God, I am so happy—I told myself.

I want to go to the Chocolab Café again tomorrow, of course, for the hot chocolate.

That night, I kept praying to God all night. Please send him to that café again. I want to see him. Just one chance, and I will definitely give him my number because I don't want to take the risk of not seeing him again. I got up from my bed, opened my drawer, and picked up my pen and diary to write the date to remember it forever.

"25th December"

I penned it down on the first left corner of the diary.

"I saw someone who could be the love of my life. There were many handsome men and beautiful women in the café, but my eyes were stuck on him. It's not like I haven't seen prettier faces than his, but the eyes are what they like, and I wish I could see him again tomorrow."

I finished writing my diary, pulled up my blankets, and went to sleep.

The next morning, I woke up, and I was smiling like an idiot, like I had found the love of my life already. I took a shower. The hot shower in the winters of Scotland is always soothing and refreshing. I made myself breakfast, poured milk and some cereal, and kept thinking and praying to see him tonight again.

My phone rang, "Hey, I am ready. See you in 5." I dropped the call, picked up my shoes, and left for college.

Leila always came to pick me up for college, and we went together to the same university in Glasgow, but in different courses.

I was studying creative writing, and Leila was studying business.

"For how long am I going to serve you as your driver, Miss Serah?" Leila asked me jokingly.

"Until I get my driving license, Sweetie"- I winked at Leila.

"This is your last drive in my car." Leila gasped.

"Oh, I have an offer for you. Take me to the college every day, and in return, I will take you to Chocolah Café every night. You drive us to the café, and I pay for the food and coffee"- I said.

"Oh, for sure" Leila said happily.

I thought in my heart that it was better to have Leila accompanied than to go alone, plus it would not look odd to myself that I went all alone to see him again.

I am always happy to spend money on people rather than doing any other favor. Money was never a problem for me. I come from a financially rich background. My father owns a university back in my town. Before my father, my grandfather owned the same university in Dundee, and he is a famous and reputed man. I was born with a golden spoon in my mouth. I enjoyed everything as a kid, and I almost had everything whenever and whatever I wanted. Being a first child, I was basically a spoiled kid. My younger sister, Lily, was totally opposite of me.

She never demanded anything more than her needs. She was a very bright student and always had her head busy with books. She was my mom's favorite because of her scores and trophies she won in school. Above all, she was brilliant in math and science, so obviously she was my parents favorite. I mean, everyone loves kids who are brilliant in mathematics and science.

On the other hand, I always hated math and science. I flunked in math almost in every class every year. I have been more into literature since I was a kid. I used to write articles for school magazines. I used to get top positions in debate and writing competitions, and obviously, my parents didn't like my study part much because I was never good in those nerdy subjects.

Even though I haven't started earning regularly, money is always in my hands. My mother is a gorgeous woman, a homemaker, and a philanthropist. She has opened a few NGO's for sewing and stitching for widows and divorcees who are not well educated. They work in institutes to sew dresses, woolen apparels, and party wear dresses on orders and supply them to the shops or directly to the customers. Ladies earn well this way and support their families.

"I am going to the library to finish my assignments. Wanna join"? Leila asked.

Yeah, sure, I will join you and read a book. it's been long since I sit in the library and read something" - I told Leila.

We both grabbed our cups of coffee and went to the library.

Our library is my favorite place in the whole university. The area is so relaxing, with large glass windows instead of walls. You can see through the greenery, beautiful huge trees, and the rustling of the wind through the glasses. The university library always gave me a sense of peace because of its infrastructure. I loved myself between thousands of books and geeks who loved reading literature.

I went straight to the fiction section to search for the book, and my eyes laid on "FORTY RULES OF LOVE BY ELIF SHAFAK". The name of the book attracted me immediately, so I picked it up, read a few lines about the book on the back cover, came back to my table, and started reading.

"FORTY RULES OF LOVE" is my favorite novel. It is the story of a middle-aged woman named Ella, who reads a manuscript about the thirteenth-century Sufi poet "RUMI" and his companion, Shams of Tabriz, and his forty rules of love and life, and how Ella's interaction with the author of the manuscript brings enormous shifts in her life.

I saw Leila indulge in her assignment from the corner of my book while sipping my coffee and told her, "Time to go home. It's 4 already".

Leila checked her watch, collected her books, and we both left together for the parking lot.

"So, are we in for tonight, or did you forget your treat"?

"Of course, I am in, Leila. Once I promise something, I fulfill it—I winked at her".

Leila and I live nearby. She lives five to six buildings away from my apartment. She dropped me off, and we decided to meet for coffee after dinner around 9 p.m.

I reached my flat, where I live alone with a house help named Mary. My father made sure that I never had to worry about other things except my studies, so he arranged a 24x7 house help for me who cleans, cooks, and does other things in the house. She is a very nice lady who I have known since I was a kid. She served my parents back in my town, so my parents trusted her enough to send her with me.

"Can I lay the table for you? You must be hungry." Her first question whenever she saw me come back from college.

Yes, sure. I am starving. Leila and I only had coffee.

"I made your favorite food—fried rice and chili chicken—Mary told me with happiness in her eyes".

Oh, Mary, you are amazing. I will go get a shower in five minutes.

I enjoyed the food and scrolled through social media. I didn't know Chocolab Café's stranger name, but I kept searching for him on Instagram, Snapchat, and Facebook. I searched for Chocolab Café's page and checked all the followers in the hope of finding his name, or it may be a picture, or it may be his friends tagged him in a photo, or it maybe they checked in with the Chocolab Cafe location. I kept looking for that one single name on Instagram among those thousands of followers of Chocolate Cafe.

I turned off Instagram and opened Snapchat while hogging over that yummy chili chicken and fried rice. I put the area name in the search location to see if people put stories there. Then I searched for a Chocolab café location on Snapchat and saw many stories, but none brought his face or name to mind. I felt sad, but I also had hope that maybe my luck would work and I would see him again tonight. It brought a sense of peace to my mind, and I turned down my phone and told Mary, "You are the best cook in the world. I am so full. Thank you, Mary."

"Your welcome, Madam" Mary said in a happy tone.

After I finished my lunch, I laid down on my carpet in my lounge. My apartment is small, but cute. My lounge is big, with a balcony attached to it. It has one L-shaped sofa with four dining chairs and a small table with a large open space (a kind of window) opened towards the kitchen. I have one large master bedroom and two bathrooms, one attached to the room and another near the main door.

My favorite spot in my flat is the carpet in my lounge with a TV in front. I never sit on a sofa but always prefer to either sit on the carpet or lay down on the carpet.

While lying down on the carpet, millions of thoughts cross my mind. Whether I will see him tonight or not, whether I should initiate talking to him or wait another few days, what if he doesn't come again to the café, and where should I find him again? I was waiting for the night to come so that I could try my luck tonight and see if he would come again or not.

"Fingers crossed". I crossed my fingers, told myself to relax, and took a nap for some time.

I woke up to the sound of my doorbell ringing. I finally managed to open my eyes and saw Leila standing directly in front of my face.

"Wake up, you crazy. We have to go for coffee." Leila yelled.

A thought of him crossed my mind again, and I sat up, rubbed my face with my hands, and checked the time on my phone.

It's 9:30 pm, and then I saw Leila drinking water, which Mary served her as a gesture of being nice whenever a guest arrives at my home.

"Give me 15 minutes, and I will go and take a shower. You go watch TV"—I said to Leila.

Okay, take your time, Leila told me. She shifted her body towards finding the remote of the TV.

I took out my favorite color, black Michael Kors tee with a cute black Zara overcoat with three golden buttons on each sleeve and six golden buttons on the front with a blue baggy jeans. I wear baggy clothes most of the time. Being skinny, I prefer to wear baggy clothes to hide my thin legs.

I love black. I have most of the tee shirts, tops, jeans, and coats in black. Black makes you feel sexy, that's what I think. I feel that black sometimes makes you mysterious or elegant. This color is deep. I have some kind of obsession with black.

I took a shower, changed into my mysterious clothes, put on my favorite Gucci perfume, and put on a little makeup. I finally took a deep breath, which I was holding for quite a few minutes. I knew that I was holding it when I managed to release it.

I went outside after getting ready and said "Hi" to Leila. She looked at me and said, "Ooh la-la, someone is looking gorgeous tonight."

"Oh, shut up" I said.

I never liked people telling me I was pretty or beautiful because I never thought that I was beautiful, so I am not good at taking compliments, but I love complimenting people. I love telling them they look good. I love telling people about little things that I notice in them, like the color of their nails, how pretty someone's hands are, or how their smile or laughter suits them. I love telling people their good things, even if it is a small detail about their appearance. But I don't like my face as much as people tell me that it's nice. My eyes are brown, and I have fair skin color with a parrot nose on it, which I hate the most about my face.

Leila and I went to the main door, and I told Mary to lock it from inside.

"We will be back in two hours"- I told Mary.

We both went to the lift and waited for the lift to come to my floor. I live on the sixth floor. It is the last floor in my building, with a swimming pool and gym area above the sixth floor.

"Let's take a selfie." Leila took out her phone, and we both posed in front of the lift mirror and clicked a few pictures.

"One more for the Snapchat streak." Leila uttered.

We went to the parking lot, took our seats, and left for the Chocolab Café. I turned down the window of the car, put my face outside to feel the chilled wind on my face, and prayed in my heart to God to send that stranger again to the café.

Chapter-2

My heart started beating at a very high rate as we came closer to the parking lot of the Chocolab Café. I felt like my heart would explode, tear my chest apart, and fall to the floor. We reached the parking lot, parked the car, and started to walk towards the stairs linked to the gate of the café. The closer I was getting to the café, the more the heartbeat was jumping up and down inside my chest. For once, I thought Leila would hear the sound of my heart beat, but nothing calmed it down. As we reached inside and searched for the table with our eyes, I felt the burning heat in my ears and cheeks and the dryness in my throat. We found a table near the staircase from where we came and sat down.

I ordered a bottle of water first. A glass of water really made me relax. I was so scared to look up and search for him through my eyes on each table that I felt I would be heartbroken if I couldn't see him. I managed to look up and search for him on the tables in front of me, then my eyes reached to the next table, and like this, one by one, I kept looking at each table attentively until it was the farthest table, and there my heart stopped beating.

The heat flushed my body again, and I felt the burning sensation in my ears and cheeks once again. I felt so happy that I wanted to scream, so happy that I wanted to tell the full café, "Look, everyone, I found him again" but I poured water again in the glass and drank to relax my hormones.

"Hey, let's order" Leila uttered.

Sure, I said, raising my right hand to get the attention of the waiter.

"One hot chocolate for me and one cappuccino for her" I told the waiter, pointing "Cappuccino" towards Leila.

Leila and I started talking about our university, and I was not at all interested in whatever Leila was talking about, so I kept nodding my head. "Yeah-Yeah" because all of my senses were lost in him. Thankfully, Leila's phone rang, and she started talking to her one and only younger sister, who lives in America.

He was sitting on the last table in the café, and I was probably on the first table. I counted the tables between us.

"Oh my God, he is eight tables away from me,"- I said in my heart.

I looked at him once and pulled my eyes down because of the stupid pressure my stupid heart was giving me. I looked at him again and checked the color of his clothes.

"Black Adidas shirt and black jeans with beige and orange Nike sneakers". I felt so happy to notice that both of us were wearing black.

"Kind of twinning today"- I told myself.

Then I looked at his face, and again, the heart started to jump on a trampoline.

His face was glowing in the moonlight. I felt like I had never seen a face glitter so much, or that it was my eyes that made his face glittery with the spark I get when I see him. Whatever the reason was, his face was glittering, and mine was sparkling. The black color suited him so much that the color of his face contrasted with his clothes so well. Big, brown, honey-dipped, charming eyes. A broad, beautiful smile with thin pink lips continuously moves while talking to his friends. His fingers are so beautiful, long, and clean that I kept looking at his hands while he was moving hands during the conversation with his friends.

"Ahh, yes, here comes the order"—Leila snapped her fingers happily.

The first sip of hot chocolate felt so good that I abruptly closed my eyes to enjoy it.

"Hot chocolate and winters are the best combination" – I told Leila.

I saw his table, and he had a barbican in his hand while others had coffee mugs. I tried to think of something to start a conversation with him or just to ask his name or where he lives, but how? He is eight tables away. How should I initiate the conversation? All the questions wrapped up my mind as I kept sipping the cup of hot chocolate without a break or putting the cup down.

I finished my hot chocolate and excused myself from Leila to go to the washroom. I went to the toilet, where one cleaner was cleaning the mirror. As I checked, both the toilet doors were locked from inside, so I waited for them to be vacant.

The cleaner and I exchanged smiles, and I suddenly thought of asking about him.

"Hey, how are you"? I asked the cleaner.

"Hello mam, I am fine", How are you? The cleaner asked me.

"I am fine, dear. Thank you," I said.

"Do you know what the name of this guy is who is sitting on the last table in black clothes?" I initiated the conversation again with the cleaner.

Cleaner smiled at me and said, "I don't know, mam. Wait, let me go and check".

I smiled and told her that he was sitting on the farthest table from the staircase, wearing full black clothes, with Barbican in hand and two other friends.

"Okay, sure" the cleaner nodded and moved outside to check.

I looked myself in the mirror of the washroom, combed my hair with my hands, darkened my lipstick a bit, and waited for the cleaner to come back.

She came back after 5 minutes, looked at my face, smiled, and said, "Yes, mam, I know him. He is our regular customer. He comes to our café almost every day with his buddies. "

I was so happy to hear this that I hugged the cleaner tight and left the bathroom.

"What took you so long in the toilet"? Leila asked.

"Umm, I got the call from my mom", I lied to Leila.

I saw him leaving with his friends. I looked at him, at his face, and I wanted to scream, "Look at me". He still didn't notice me. He didn't notice how badly someone's heart rate increased when he crossed my chair towards the staircase.

Soon after he left, I kept telling Leila to let's get up and go home, but she was so busy scrolling Snapchat and sending streaks that she didn't notice that I don't want to sit in this café anymore when he is not here.

It is so boring without him. This café is so damn boring without him. It felt like all the glitter and sparkle of the night had gone with him.

Finally, Leila said, "Let's go, sweetie. It's late. We have class tomorrow."

"Oh, finally someone said what I was trying to say for the last fifteen minutes"- I told Leila.

We both smiled and drove our way home.

There was something beautiful about that night—something fresh, something fragrant. I felt like there was happiness all around. Trees are smiling with me, the wide sky is smiling with me, and people are smiling with me.

Leila dropped me home, and we said good-bye to each other. I reached home and saw Mary watching TV. I went to my bedroom, changed my clothes, and got into bed. I pulled my diary out again and wrote a few lines.

Date: December 26, 2020

"I saw him again. He looked marvelous. I wish I could come and talk to you. I wish I could ask you about your name and where you live. I wish to see you again tomorrow".

I finished scribbling a few lines and put the diary back in my drawer.

I lay down in my bed while looking out the huge side window of my bed, which faces the road and the vast sky full of stars. I always sleep with curtains pulled back because I love looking at the sky and the millions of stars shining in the darkness of night. I love waking up to the fresh brightness of the morning, the sun throwing its shine, and making the entire room lustrous.

I hugged my pillow and turned myself towards the window while looking at the sky, smiling like an idiot, reminiscing over the time spent in the café, and dozed off. I don't know when.

Chapter-3

I woke up with Leila's phone around 8:30 when she told me she was going to pick me up in 20 minutes. I dropped the call and went straight to the bathroom, took a quick shower, and changed into my blue jeans and blue Nike sweatshirt. I asked Mary to clean my blue Jordan 1 Retro High. I have a fetish for shoes, especially Air Jordan's. I love buying shoes, and I love people who gift me shoes. Everyone in my family and friends knows about my obsession with shoes.

I ate my cereal fast, which Mary made ready, and left for college with Leila.

"Hey, do you want to go to the Chocolab Café again tonight?" It was my first question to Leila as soon as I saw her face.

"No, sweetie, I am sorry. I have my test tomorrow. I gotta study."

"Oh, okay, I said with a low face".

I went to my class when the professor said, "We have a Creative Writing Masterclass today. A mock test where you will be given a topic to write an article on in not more than 1000 words."

I already said that because Leila is not coming to the café, how will I go tonight to see him? I don't have a car. I asked myself while looking at my laptop screen, waiting for the professor to give us a topic to write about.

My topic was "Growth versus Fixed Mindsets. Which is better, and why?"

I tried to think of the first few words to start the writing, but my mind was already occupied with "Whether I will see him tonight or not." Initializing a few lines to start writing a prompt is always important because that's how you structure your whole article. If you get a hold of the starting lines, you can easily write an article in flow. And I was stuck because of the thought of tonight and couldn't get the one word to start my writing.

I waited for the lecture to finish, didn't submit my article that day, and left the class.

I joined Leila in the library, and I picked up the "FORTY RULES OF LOVE" again and started flipping pages without any interest in reading when I saw 19th RULE OF LOVE - "Fret not where the road will take you. Instead, concentrate on the first step. That is the hardest part, and that is what you are responsible for. Once you take that step, let everything do what it naturally does, and the rest will follow. Don't go with the flow. Be the flow.*"

I closed the book, put my head down on the table, and started thinking about tonight.

"Why the hell can I not think of anything else other than seeing him?" I asked myself angrily.

I will go alone. I told myself. I will book a cab and go alone.

I took a sigh of relief. My face got a bit happy. I opened my laptop and started thinking about "GROWTH VS. FIXED MINDSET". I started typing, and when I finished writing my article, I sent the PDF to my professor. I will not get any marks because it was a surprise test, but at least I submitted. "It's better than not writing anything at all." I told myself.

I waited for the night to come. Mary served me my evening tea, and I searched for the Chocolab café again on Instagram and checked the story's official page to see him. But I couldn't find anything related to him. I decided to ask his name today. I decided in my heart that if I saw him alone, I would go and talk to him. Ask for his name, and ask where he lived.

I changed my clothes to go to the café. I wore a red sweater by keeping in mind to talk to him tonight. Red is the color of love, so I chose to wear a red sweater with blue jeans and my AIR JORDAN (BLACK FIRE RED). I wore my favorite Tom Ford Oud Wood perfume. Perfumes and shoes are my most favorite things in the whole world, and I have a huge collection of both. I did minimal makeup. I was never interested in makeup. I never liked people who put on a lot of makeup. I like it to be natural. Natural face, natural body. So, I never put on a lot of makeup. I popped a mint gum into my mouth and booked a cab for the café. My phone rang soon, and after three minutes, I booked a cab. I left my apartment for the road where the cab was parked. Cab service is amazing in this city. They always reach within two to three minutes of booking.

My heart was so restless on the way to the café. Firstly, I was going alone for the first time, and secondly, I had the thought of talking to him tonight. I put my headphones on and started listening to music. The cab driver dropped me at the entrance of the café, and I took the stairs to reach the main area. I looked up for the table to sit at. I took the last seat near the stairs, as usual, and ordered my hot chocolate. I looked and traced the whole café but couldn't find him. I felt a bit sad with the thought of not seeing him today, but I decided to wait until my hot chocolate finished. And there I saw him, this time only two tables away. He felt so near that I could look into his face so easily. My heart started to jump with happiness. He was alone that night. He didn't come with his friends, and as usual, he had his coffee mug in his hands. I wanted to ask him what kind of coffee he likes to drink. I was thinking about what to ask him if I got the chance to talk to him tonight. I took a sip of my hot chocolate and looked at him while putting the cup down. I saw him waving at the waiter for the bill as he finished his coffee. I asked another waiter to bring my bill because I wanted to go to the parking lot before him so that I could talk. I paid the bill, walked towards the parking lot, and waited for him to come.

He came down after five minutes, and I felt my heart leaving my body.

I saw him.

"Hey" - I said.

"Hey", he smiled and replied.

"What is your name?" I asked hesitantly.

"Cooper, it's Cooper" he replied with a little smile.

"Do we know each other?" I haven't seen you before, Cooper said.

"No, we don't. Though I come here every day."

"Oh, that's great. See you soon." Cooper replied.

We shook hands and said, "Good night", and he left. I was there at the gate for the next ten minutes, trying to recover from the meeting and the handshake. His soft and warm hand. I looked at my hand and smiled like crazy. I booked the cab, waited for the next four minutes, and left for home.

I reached home and smiled throughout my time, from café to home to my bedroom. I changed into my pajamas, curled up in bed, and took out my diary to write about my first meeting.

Date: 27th December

Oh my God, I can't believe he touched me. It was just a shaking hand, but it was amazing. I talked to him, and I was lost in his big brown eyes. He told me, "SEE YOU" which means I have more chances to see him. I am so happy tonight.

I put the diary back in its place, wrapped the blanket around my face, and slept very well that night.

I woke up to the alarm the next morning. I checked the phone, and it was 8:30 a.m. I woke up with a smile and a very good mood. I took a shower and left for the university without having breakfast, but I smiled all the way to my university. The day felt beautiful and different. I couldn't stop thinking about him. Even if I wanted to stop thinking about Cooper, I started to think more. I decided to go to the café tonight also, but this time alone. I didn't even ask Leila to join me because I wanted him to see me. I wanted to see him. I waited for my lectures to finish and joined Leila in the university cafeteria for coffee and brunch.

"Where are you lost? You didn't answer my WhatsApp message last night." Leila mumbled.

"I slept early last night. I saw your message in the morning"—I lied to Leila.

"Let's go to Chocolab Café tonight. I miss the coffee there."- Leila asked.

"I don't think I can join you. I have to finish my assignment by tonight"—I lied to Leila again.

I didn't want Leila to come with me. I was not ready to answer her unlimited questions about Cooper. How did I meet him? Why did I talk to him, and where did I see him? I was not ready to answer all these questions yet, so I lied to her.

I went back to my home. Mary cooked me chili garlic noodles. I stuffed myself and took a nap. I loved taking naps in the afternoon when the classes got over early on some days.

I woke up to my phone ringing with my sister's call. She calls me almost every day just to blabber. We are very close to each other. From choosing clothes for each other to asking for recipes for food, we always stay in touch, either through WhatsApp or a phone call. We talked again about the latest bags by Louis Vuitton and how much my sister liked and wanted one. I talked to her for 45 minutes, then took a shower.

I went to my study table, opened my laptop, and tried to focus on my assignments. Every time I try to focus, I get more lost in Cooper's thoughts. I kept staring at my screen with all the thoughts of him, shaking hands with him last night to think of seeing him again tonight.

I told Mary to iron my clothes, and she looked puzzled. She wanted to ask him where I was going every night but couldn't.

I got ready with my pretty black hoodie and grey jeans. God! I love black.

I took a book with me and booked a cab for the café. I told Mary I would be back in 2 hours and left.

When I reached the café, I saw him sitting near the stairs, and he was the first face I saw when I entered the café. My heart thumped so badly. He waved at me, and I waved at him back.

He was alone, and I was alone. We exchanged a few glances with a smile. He looked so perfect, so neat, and so gorgeous. Does he always look so good, anytime, all the time? I asked myself.

I thought of giving my number to him. But how? I cannot go directly and give him my number among so many people. I thought of a few ideas but couldn't get one.

I went to the washroom again and saw the same cleaner who was there before, who told me Cooper is a regular customer. My mind suddenly clicked, and I pulled down a tissue sheet. I asked her for a pen. She went outside and brought a pen. I wrote down my number and my name with a (I met you in parking) note. I asked the cleaner to give it to Cooper.

I didn't order anything that night. I told the cleaner to give this tissue to Cooper when I left. I left soon after talking to her and kept looking at my phone to ring or send a message.

When I reached home, I saw his message, and I literally started jumping out of happiness in my bedroom.

"Hey, a waiter gave me this number" he texted.

"Hey, I didn't find any other way to share my number with you. I'm sorry if you mind it" - I replied.

"No worries, that's fine" Cooper answered.

I didn't know what to say more, so I said, "Good night, Cooper."

"Good night, Serah" he replied.

I took out my diary.

Date: December 28

Cooper messaged me. I hope you know how much I like you, Cooper. I am so happy that you messaged me.

I closed the diary and went to sleep.

Every morning felt like a new morning. I felt like I was born today. Every morning felt so fresh. I didn't know anything about him. I didn't know if he had a girlfriend. I didn't know if he was married or what he did. I never thought all this time about his relationship status. I was going so crazy for him that nothing else mattered to me except him.

I didn't go to college. I told Leila I didn't have a class. I didn't want to think about anything else that day. I didn't want any other thoughts in my mind except

Cooper's. I waited for night all day. I wanted the night to come early. I waited for his message. I wanted to talk, but I didn't want to sound desperate, as I had already shown too much.

I saw my phone, and it was 8 p.m. I jumped out of the sofa, got ready, and left for the café. I took my novel with me. I went early because I couldn't stay at home. I couldn't stay without seeing him. I reached the café, and he was not there. I checked my phone, and it was still 8.45 p.m. He usually comes at 9, so I waited. I didn't order anything yet and kept myself busy reading my novel. I looked up after a few minutes, and he was there. Three tables away. He smiled. I smiled, and I looked down into my book again. He was alone.

My phone rang, and it was his text. "Come join me," he said.

"You come and sit with me," I replied.

I saw his face. He was smiling at his phone. In a few minutes, he came to my table. He was sitting directly in front of me, and I couldn't be any happier. I saw his face, and I got lost in his eyes. His face hypnotized me so much that I forgot the whole world. I forgot that I exist.

"So, what do you do, Serah?" Cooper asked.

"I am studying creative writing" I replied.

"Oh, you are a writer"—he smiled and said.

"I wish I could one day. Writing is my passion. I want to write a book someday"- I replied.

"What do you do? Do you live near this area?" I asked him.

"I am the owner of this café. This café is mine, and my house is nearby" he answered.

"Oh, really? The cleaner told me you are a regular customer" I said.

"Maybe she got confused. He smiled at me."

"So, what is your favorite drink as the owner of this café? I will try that" I said.

"Umm, try the lemon mint mojito. That's my personal favorite" he said.

I ordered a lemon mint mojito, and he had his coffee.

"Well, it's yummy, very tasty," I told Cooper.

He got a call from someone. He excused himself that night and left. I suddenly hated the lemon mint mojito. I left half of the glass unfinished and booked a cab to go back home.

"Sorry to leave early. I had something urgent come up. I hope you reached safely"- my phone blinked with his text message.

I smiled and replied back, "No problem, I am about to reach in 5 minutes."

I put my phone down, looked outside the window, and felt nice in my heart and mind.

Chapter-4

I was waiting for Leila in the university's library to join me after her class. I picked up "FORTY RULES OF LOVE" and read the 10th rule – *"The quest for love changes us. There is no seeker among those who search for love who has not matured along the way. The moment you start looking for love, you start to change within and without."*

I liked the book, and I liked these rules. I think they make sense somehow. I closed the book and thought about this 10th rule. Yes, it's true. The quest for love changes us. Love means to feel a change in yourself and feel happy about it. My thoughts were disturbed soon by a voice.

"Hey idiot, where have you been"?

"Hey Leila, I took a day off from seeing you. My eyes got tired of seeing you twice a day." I winked at her.

"You asshole"—she laughed, and we both walked towards the classrooms.

"See you after the class" high-fived each other and decided to meet later at the parking.

Everyone in my class is always busy, either writing something or reading novels. I kind of love the atmosphere of reading and writing. I love checking out the novels my classmates read and reading the writing prompts. The room is always full of positive energy with future passionate writers. I saw Leila after the class, and she invited me for dinner at her place. She learned a new pasta recipe and wanted to try it on me. I didn't want to accept because I wanted to go to Chocolab Café to see Cooper. I felt bad for Leila, so I didn't say no to her and accepted her invitation.

We decided to meet at 8 p.m. I didn't want to go, but I had to go to eat her new pasta. I checked my phone. There was no message from Cooper. I want him to message me. I want him to talk to me all the time. I want him to tell me that he is thinking about me as much as I am thinking about him. Unfortunately, the phone was blank.

Leila's home is near my home, so I decided to take a walk to her home. I bought a cake from a bakery and walked towards her home. I won't be able to see him tonight. That's what kept making me sad until I reached her home. I was kind of angry at Leila for inviting me, but I didn't show her.

Leila had a cute, small studio apartment. A large room that included a kitchen, television lounge, and dining area. All together in one place in one hall.

I reached her home in 5-7 minutes.

As soon as she saw my face, she handed me a big bowl of vegetables to chop down for pasta.

"So, you invited me to cut these vegetables."

"Yes, I love it when your guess is almost right," she said.

"Chop these fast. I am making white sauce and boiling the pasta," Leila said.

I gave her a bad look. She smiled and pointed her finger towards the vegetable bowl.

Leila has a boyfriend who is studying in America, and she cooks while talking to him for the full hour. I was thinking, what is there to talk about for hours?

Then I thought of Cooper and realized I could talk to him all day, every single minute.

I went to the kitchen, gave chopped veggies to Leila, and asked her to cut the phone with the movement of my hand. She put the phone down and finished cooking.

"Come, Sweetie, the best pasta in the world is ready" master chef Leila said.

I took a bite, and it was the most delicious pasta I'd had in a long time.

"Ben is coming to the UK next week"- Leila told me excitedly.

Wow, that's amazing. Have a great time with him.

My phone rang. It was Cooper's WhatsApp text.

My heart skipped a beat.

"Hey, aren't you coming to the café tonight?"

"No, I am at my friend's place for dinner." I texted back.

Cooper doesn't have any idea how this one message made me so happy.

I started to smile like an idiot, and my mood got so fresh.

Sometimes a single person can make such a difference in your life, I wonder.

"Will you come tomorrow", another text from Cooper.

"Yes, hopefully," I replied.

I was in such a happy mood after his message that I asked Leila to watch a movie with me. We decided to watch "GONE GIRL." Leila made green tea for both of us, and we both enjoyed the movie. I kept looking at my phone every now and then, hoping he might message me again.

Hope is a dangerous thing for a woman like me to have—but I have it.

Next morning, I woke up early in the morning for the jog. I have always loved gymming, jogging, and exercising. I love taking long walks. I love mornings. I have always been a morning person. When I came back home from jogging, I checked my phone. It was

Cooper's message on the screen. The morning never felt better.

"Hey, good morning. Let's catch up today at 11 a.m., if you are free. I will pick you up. Share your location."

Oh, my goodness! I screamed out of happiness.

Mary got scared and came back running to my room. "Madam, are you alright?"

"Yes, Mary, I am super fine. I just got my finger stuck in the door." I lied.

"Oh, Madam, I will bring ice for your finger" - poor Mary said.

"I am fine, Mary. Don't worry - I said."

I thought about what to say for the next fifteen minutes. I didn't want to sound desperate to meet him, though I was really desperate to see him.

"Okay Cooper. See you at 11"—I replied and shared my location.

I drank two glasses of water to calm myself down. God has been too kind to me for the last few days. I looked up and said, Thank you, God.

The first thing I did was message Leila, "Don't come to pick me up. I won't be going to the university today, not feeling well."

"Okay babe, take care," she answered.

I took out my black floral maxi dress with pretty heels to wear. I wanted to look my best for him. I wanted Cooper to see me not with his eyes but with his heart. I was ready before the time. I couldn't wait to see him, and I couldn't wait to go on a drive with him.

"My phone rang exactly at 11 a.m. Hey, come down. I am here."

"Coming," I replied.

My heart was bouncing. I never felt such a rapid heartbeat before.

I reached down and looked out for his car.

"Hey, he screamed from his car."

I waved back and walked towards his car.

I loved his car and his black jaguar. It was as pretty as Cooper's eyes.

"Know any place to go?" he asked.

"No idea, you choose," I said.

We went to another new café. The café was gorgeous, near the sea. We took our seats and ordered coffee.

"So, what do you do in your free time?" I asked.

"I love baking" he answered.

"Wow, being a man, that's very cool. I would love to eat something from Cooper's bakery," I said.

Ha-ha—sure, he answered.

"What about you? What do you do?" He asked.

"I read. I am a bookworm. I read and write. I want to become a writer someday"- I said.

"Fantastic, write a book on me one day." He said.

"Of course, one day"- I answered.

Cooper had an amazing face. A face that made me crazy from day one. There was something very charming about him. When you love someone, you don't find anyone attractive. There were many other handsome men, more handsome than Cooper, but I didn't like anyone except him. I couldn't move my eyes from his face. I didn't want to look anywhere except at his face. I saw him that day properly.

He had the most beautiful, deep eyes. Eyes that light up the whole room, eyes that brighten the darkness. There was something deep about his eyes. Lonely eyes. He had an amazing facial structure. I loved his chin. There was a small line exactly under his lower lip on his chin, which I found very attractive. I wanted to kiss under his lower lip on the chin, exactly on that sweet small line. Thin lips, but gorgeous. Cute little nose.

We didn't talk much that day, which may be because we were meeting like that for the first time. We looked at each other every now and then. He looked at me quite a few times, and every time he looked at me, I felt weak. We enjoyed each other's company that day. I enjoyed the silence with him. It was comfortable to sit with him like that.

Cooper and I left together. He asked to drop me back at my home. I spent two hours with him, and I never knew time would pass so fast. I wanted to meet him again. I didn't want to ask him to meet me tomorrow. I wanted him to ask me, Hey, let's meet up tomorrow again.

My home came, and he didn't ask what I wanted to hear, so I left my goggles in his car on my seat. Thankfully, he didn't notice my goggles and left for work.

I reached home happily. Very happy, very excited.

"You forgot your goggles in my car"- he messaged.

I smiled. I left it on purpose, I thought.

"Oh, I am sorry. Keep it. I will take it some other time"- I answered.

"It was nice meeting you," I replied.

"Same here,"- Cooper messaged back.

I opened my diary.

Date: 2nd January

I loved meeting with Cooper today. I wish he could see in my eyes how much I have started loving him. Sitting in his car with him was the best part of today. There was nobody else except me and him. I loved going with him, and spending time with him in his car was the best. I wish I could spend more of my time with him in his car than at any other café.

I put the diary back in its place and relaxed on my sofa.

Chapter-5

'Oh my god, my mom is calling' I saw my phone and thought about how I had to answer her if she asked why I didn't go to university.

"Hey Mom, I said, how are you doing?"

"I am fine, my sweetie. Your dad and I miss you, so we are planning to visit you"- she said.

"Oh, that's great" with a dead heart, thinking, how would I see Cooper if my parents were here".

"Aren't you happy that we are coming to see you?" My mother asked, hearing nothing from my side"

No, no, I am so happy. I just have a bit of a headache," I said.

"So, when are you planning to come" - I asked my mother.

"This weekend"—she replied and said bye to me.

I checked my calendar on the phone. Today is Wednesday. I still have two days to see Cooper until Saturday.

"Wow, madame, sir, and ma'am are coming this weekend," Mary asked happily.

Yes, they are, I replied.

Mary started telling me what dishes she would cook when mom and dad were here.

I wanted to see Cooper tonight. I messaged him.

"Hey Cooper, if you are free tonight, can you give me my goggles back? I have a migraine, and I have to wear goggles when I go out in the sun. Tomorrow I have class."

"Yes, of course." Cooper replied in 1 minute.

I felt happy that I would see him tonight as well. Seeing Cooper two times in a day, wow.

I got ready for tonight. We decided to go to the same café. I have also started to fall in love with Chocolab Café.

At exactly 9 p.m., I was there. I waited for Cooper. I was always early before him in excitement.

"Where are you?" he messaged me.

"Already in café", I replied.

"Cool, I will be there in 5 minutes. Order pizza. I am hungry"- he replied.

"Okay" – I said.

I waved at the waiter to come to my table and take my order.

"Yes, mam, what can I get for you?" asked the waiter.

"One chicken pizza and two Coke" I ordered.

I saw Cooper coming. In white Nike sweatshirt and blue jeans. He looked fresh. Fresh as daisy.

We shake hands and take our seats.

"Sorry for keeping you waiting. I was stuck in traffic".

"No problem. It's okay"- I replied.

Our pizza arrived with two Cokes. Pizza looked delicious. Fluffy pan pizza with cheese-laden chunks of chicken. I felt hungry.

Cooper sliced one piece of pizza with a pizza slicer and served it on my plate.

"Thank you," I said.

The melt-in-the mouth pizza tastes amazing.

"My parents are coming over this weekend"- I told Cooper.

"Hey, that's great" Cooper replied.

"It's not great. You should know this, Cooper. I won't be able to see you for a week, I thought to myself."

"Yes, it's great," I answered.

"Bring them to the café. I would like to meet them."

"Sure, I will try"- I said.

"Who else is there in your family, and what did you study?" I asked Cooper, as I had never asked him about his family, home, or profession.

"I have my mom and dad. I don't have any siblings. My parents live in Bromley, and my father looks out for another café. I live alone here, and I studied business"- he said.

"Oh, that's amazing. Living alone is wonderful." I said.

"Yes, sometimes my mom comes to visit me and stay with me," he said.

I took a sip of my coke and thought, what if Cooper brings girls home? He lives alone, he is rich, and he is handsome. I am sure he must have too many girls after him.

"Do you have a girlfriend?" I asked him.

"I am single right now"- he said.

"Right now," doesn't sound good to me. It means he had girlfriend in past. Maybe a year ago, or a month ago or until last week. I couldn't imagine Cooper with any other girl even if it's in his past.

"Do you have a boyfriend? You are still a student. You must have lots of guys around you"- he asked me.

Yes, I have too many male friends from university but nobody is there to tag as "boyfriend." They are just friends, not my type.

"So, what's your type"- he asked me.

"You are my type". My soul saw you and it kind of went like 'OH THERE YOU ARE,' I have been looking for you- I murmured in my heart."

Umm... "When I look at him and my heart say- if the life is repeated a thousand times still you, you and again you- I told him"

Cooper laughed and said – "that's deep."

It was 11 p.m., and I told Cooper I wanted to go back home. I have a class early morning.

"I am booking the cab"- I said.

"No, leave it. I have your goggles in my car. I will give you and drop you back," he said.

And we both left for the parking lot.

I saw his car and thought how much I loved sitting with him in it. I feel safe in his car without people, without crowds, and without any noise from outside the world.

Cooper stopped his car near my home. He gave me back my goggles from the dashboard of his car. He handed me over the goggles, and as soon as I held the goggles, he pulled my hands, which were holding the goggles, closer to his mouth. He looked at my mouth as much as I was looking at his mouth. I loved this moment of closeness. He came closer to my mouth and touched my lips with his. I felt the softness of his lips on my lips.

I felt the warmth of his mouth on mine. He held my face in between his hands and kissed my lips. I dropped the goggles down and put my hands around his face. I kissed him back. I put my tongue in his mouth, and he sucked my tongue softly, making me breathe faster. I opened my eyes to see his face while kissing. His eyes were closed, and his mouth was busy sucking my tongue. I sucked his lips harder. I loved his heavy breathing in my mouth. I didn't want him to stop. I want him to eat me the whole night.

He stopped and looked at my face. We both smiled and kissed each other again.

He hugged me softly, and we bid good night to each other.

I started jumping, thinking about him kissing me in my room. Oh god, I can't believe we kissed. I couldn't stop smiling. This was the happiest day of my life. I am already in love with Cooper.

Date: 2nd January

I love you, Cooper. I am madly, crazily in love with you. Kiss me more, kiss me every day, and kiss me every minute and every second. I miss you already. I wish you could see in my eyes when you looked at my face how honestly and truly I am in love with you.

I put the diary back in the drawer.

I had mixed feelings after writing everything in the diary. I was happy because we kissed and sad because I love Cooper and he doesn't know about it. Maybe he doesn't love me. Maybe it was just a normal kiss for him.

Chapter-6

I woke up next morning with a sad face because last night's kiss left a question mark on my thoughts about Cooper and his feelings.

I had my tea while thinking of Cooper. I don't know why I think of him so much. I can't think of anything else except him. It annoys me sometimes how madly I have fallen for him. I called Leila and asked to meet her for some grocery shopping. I also didn't want to stay alone and keep thinking about Cooper.

"Let's go shopping. Pick me up in one hour if you are free"- I texted Leila.

She replied back in 2 minutes. "Sure, I will pick you up. Let's meet."

I love people who reply fast. I feel like they are interested in you. They give you importance.

Leila and I went to the nearest mall for shopping. I bought some of my mom's favorite food. She loves bakery products like me. I bought a few cakes, freshly baked bread and croissants, a tray of eggs, and some cereal.

We stopped for coffee in a café. All this time, I kept thinking about Cooper. I think of him while buying bread. I think of him while talking to the salesman in the grocery shop, while stuffing my trolley with groceries, at the bill counter, at the coffee shop while ordering coffee, and while talking to Leila. There is not even a single second pass when I don't think of him, when I don't miss him. And I wonder if he thinks of me too. Not as much as I do, but maybe a little? While driving alone to work, what does he think of me? We kissed in his car, and I was sitting on the next seat with him. While in the café, he sees everyone there but not me. Do you think of me, Cooper? I wondered.

"Is everything okay? Why are you so quiet?" Leila questioned.

"Yes, I am fine. I am just thinking about what else I have to do for my parents to make their stay comfortable"- I lied to Leila.

I wasn't thinking about them. I was thinking about that one person who occupied my mind and my soul.

I reached home and thanked Leila for accompanying me.

"Come up, have lunch with me."

"Some other time, babe, gotta rush"- she replied.

And we said good-bye to each other.

I came home and gave the stuff to Mary to keep it in its place.

My phone rang, and it was Cooper.

There was relief on my face and in my heart. My crankiness and anger went away in one minute just by seeing his name on my phone.

But I didn't pick up the call. I don't want to answer him because I am upset.

He called again, and I didn't pick up this time either.

I went straight to bed and pulled the blanket up to my face.

"Should I call him back or wait for his call or message again?" I started biting my lips and thinking about what to do.

I put my phone on my side table and closed my eyes to think.

My phone rang again, and it was his text.

"Hey, I have been calling you, but you didn't pick. I hope you are okay."

I kept looking at the message for another five minutes to see what to answer.

"Hey, been busy with assignments. All good! How about you?" I replied back.

I am fine. I am baking something. Wanna try this master chef's yummy cake?

I smiled at his message.

"Yeah, sure, let me see the master chef's culinary talent. I hope I don't get upset stomach"- I replied back with a wink emoji.

"LOL, I will pick you up at 9 p.m. tonight"- he replied.

"Sure, done" I answered.

I got happy thinking about that Cooper thought about me while baking. He remembered that I love eating cakes and bakery stuff. All the frustration I had went away with one call.

This is how much he affects me.

I was happy and nervous to go to his home, though I always felt safe with him.

I ordered a bottle of wine to take, as I don't like to show up at someone's house empty-handed.

I took a shower, put on my favorite lavender body moisturizer, a bit of makeup, and cherry-flavored lip balm. I dressed up in casual black cargo pants and a black tee shirt with my hair neatly tied up in a bun.

Exactly at 9, Cooper messaged, "Hey, come down."

"Coming in two minutes, I replied."

I grabbed my purse and the bottle of wine and left for the parking area.

I waited for Cooper for the next two minutes. Maybe he messaged me before reaching me, and I moved down too fast. hahaahah.. I laughed at myself.

He came within 2 minutes.

We said 'hey' to each other, and he drove to his house. I love his eyes. I saw many eyes, but his eyes are my favorites.

Cooper's house is really close to the café, maybe five minute drive from the café and 20 minutes from my home.

He parked the car and guided me towards the main door to the lift. He lives on the first floor. He unlocked his door and removed his shoes at the doorstep. I did the same, removed my shoes, and followed him to his living room.

He has a beautiful, bright house. All glittery and shiny. Kitchen near the main door with a big window open towards the dining table in the living room. Cream sofas with huge sofa pillows and cute pink curtains, a large golden table in the center with two lamps on the table, and a TV in front. He had plants in his living room as well, which means he likes plants and flowers as well.

He removed his jacket, and I noticed his very sexy, bulgy arms and took my eyes off of his arms in another direction. He is sexy.

He has an amazing face, an amazing body, and amazing hands. I wish for his heart to be amazing as well, because this is what matters the most in the end.

He brought the cake to the table.

"Oh nice, its lotus biscoff?" I asked him.

"Yep, lotus biscoff cheesecake, he said while giving me a slice of cake on a plate."

"Oh my god, Cooper, that's scrumptious." I said this after taking the first bite.

"Really?" He asked.

"I loved it. It's better than any café in London, I said.

Cooper sat down near me on the same sofa, turned on the TV, and played some songs on YouTube. We were both enjoying the cheesecake that he made and watching TV.

His knees touched mine accidentally, and his hands touched mine unintentionally. I loved that feeling.

I loved how close we are to each other, and I loved how we were alone without any other crowd, like in a café. I love how Cooper is with me alone. I finished my cake and put the plate down on the table.

There was something in that moment of loneliness with him. Every time his hand touched mine, I got the feeling of electricity in my backbone.

"Can I hold your hand?" Cooper asked.

I nodded with my head.

He held my hand. My hand was in his hand, and we kept looking at TV.

He started to touch the middle of my palm with his thumb while holding my hand. It felt good. I felt nice.

He kept rubbing my hand gently with his fingers and turned his face towards me from TV. He came closer to my face and pressed his lips against mine. I closed my eyes and felt his warm lips on mine. He gently and slowly kissed my lips again and again. He lifted me up and made me sit on his lap. I looked at his face closely for the first time. He is charming. He makes me crazy. I held his face between my hands. He put his hands into my hair, and we kissed each other madly. He sucked my lips, my mouth, and my tongue, and I loved every bit of it. I rolled my tongue into his mouth and kissed him crazily. I pulled his lower lip softly with my teeth, bit his lips gently, and sucked on his lips again and again.

He moaned, "Oh baby, I love you" in my mouth.

"I stopped kissing him and looked into his eyes. I love you, Cooper" I said.

I kissed him again. "I love you so much"- I said while kissing him into his mouth.

His hand started moving on my back, and I kept kissing him like it was the last time I was kissing him.

His lips moved to my neck, he rubbed his lips slowly on the left side of my neck, and I grabbed his hair and pushed myself on him. He started sucking on my neck, and I kept hugging him tightly while enjoying every bit of it.

"Oh, Cooper" I moaned.

"He was breathing heavily on my neck."

He made my tongue wet with his tongue. He rubbed his tongue hard all over my neck, and I kept moaning and asking for more.

His hands touched my boobs. I licked his earlobe, and his hands were on my boobs, softly pressing them on my shirt.

He put his hands under my shirt and pressed my breasts again over my bra. I kissed his neck while hugging him tightly.

He unhooked my bra under my shirt and held my boobs in his hands. I moaned like a mad woman. "ahh Cooper, I love you."

He rubbed my nipples with his thumb, making me crazier than ever. I moaned again in his ear.

He removed my shirt, and I removed his shirt, and we hugged each other.

He put one of his fingers in his mouth, made it wet, and put his saliva on my nipples, making my nipples wet and soft. He held my left boob in his hand and licked my nipple with the tip of his tongue while rubbing another nipple with the finger of another hand.

I pushed his face more into my boob, asking him to suck it more. He sucked my nipple, and he sucked my boob, making it so wet. He kept rubbing my nipple up and down with his town, making me groan with pleasure.

He did the same on my other boob. We both moaned madly.

He put his hand down on my pants and touched my pussy.

"Your pussy is warm, I can feel its heat on my hand," he said into my ear.

I smiled and kissed his nose.

He opened the button on my pants and slipped his hand over my pants. He moaned in excitement while feeling the hotness of my pussy over my panty. He slowly rubbed his hand on my pussy making me mad and crazy, asking him to get inside me.

He put his saliva on his fingers from his mouth and rubbed it inside my pants, making me more wet. He touched my clit with his fingers, and I screamed in pleasure.

Oh, Cooper, put your fingers inside – I said.

He slipped his fingers inside my pussy and we both moaned with passion.

"Push more and move your fingers inside." I told him.

He put inside this time his two fingers and moved them inside me, touching and rubbing my clitoris. He started moving his fingers fast and hard inside, and I pulled his hair out of pleasure until I reached my orgasm.

He kissed my forehead, we hugged each other, and we slept that night on the sofa. I loved the warmth of his body, I loved how close he was to me, and I loved how I felt his breath on my neck. I loved everything about Cooper. I love Cooper.

Chapter-7

I woke up the next morning in his arms. I never slept that well. I felt safe in his arms. I looked up at his face, his eyes closed. He looked perfect while sleeping. I admired his face, gazed at his lips, and smiled. Every part of my body felt happy. I felt love for him in my bones. He opened his eyes, looked at my face with those honey eyes, and kissed my lips.

"Good morning, beautiful" he said.

"Good morning, handsome" I replied.

"Freshen up yourself. I will make you coffee" Cooper said.

And what would you like to eat for breakfast?

"I love pancakes." I giggled.

Sure, pancakes for the lady.

I got up and went to bathroom to brush my teeth.

I found the bathroom cute and tidy, with clean golden tiles on wall, a bathtub where I imagined cooper and me taking a bath together. His perfumes, hair gel, shaving kit everything was set at the bathroom rack accordingly.

"Breakfast is ready"- Cooper yelled.

I went outside the room to the dining table and saw the table set with yummy pancakes laden with strawberries and banana, two coffee mugs, sandwiches and fruits.

"You did too much" I said to Cooper.

"I am hungry, I will finish it all"- he said.

"You really are an amazing chef Cooper, pancakes taste amazing. I can never cook such amazing food" I told Cooper.

"You don't need to cook. Just tell me whenever you want to eat and I will cook for you"- he replied.

I smiled and finished the breakfast.

Cooper dropped me home around 10 a.m. to my house.

I reached my home and Mary started interrogating me like an FBI.

"Where were you all night madam"- she asked.

"I was at Leila's place, Mary. Don't worry"- I replied.

"But why did you sleep at her house, Madam?" another question came from her side.

"Because mom dad are coming tomorrow and I will not get to spend as much time with her. Relax Mary" I said.

I went into my room and got straight to my bed, thinking about everything that happened between me and Cooper. I wanted to take a shower and go to college to attend my 1 p.m. lecture, but I didn't take a shower because I didn't want Cooper's touch to go away. I didn't want to stop smelling like him. I didn't want to wash off his saliva from my body so I decided to stay in his smell. I decided not to shower.

I took out my pen and diary.

3rd January

Cooper made love with me. I am on cloud nine today. I cannot believe I spent a night at his home in his bed and in his arms. It was heaven. I wish to spend every night with you Cooper. I am in love with you. I breathe you, I smell you, I love you.

"Do you want to eat something madam"- Mary yelled from the kitchen.

"No Mary. I am full. Just cook something for a lunch"- I said.

"Sure madam"- Mary answered.

I opened my laptop to finish the assignment but ended up staring at the screen and thinking about how passionately we kissed last night. I miss Cooper so much. I turned off the laptop, picked up my phone and messaged him.

"Hey Cooper, I miss you."

"Hey baby, I miss you too. Cannot wait to see you"- he replied back.

I love how he make me feel important, how fast he replies me back.

I smiled at my phone and texted him back.

"See you soon."

"See you very soon" he replied.

I felt agitated thinking about my parents coming tomorrow—God knows for how many days? I was not happy because it would be hard to meet Cooper. I felt annoyed to think they would be here all the time with me.

I want them to meet Cooper. I want Cooper to meet them. I want them to like him. I want him to like them.

I got up to get ready for my evening class. I missed a few of my classes in order to meet Cooper, and I took extra classes for the lectures I missed.

I reached college early and went straight to the library, picked up the same novel that I was reading, and ended up reading Rule No. 13, which says:

"TRY NOT TO RESIST THE CHANGES, WHICH COME YOUR WAY. INSTEAD, LET LIFE LIVE THROUGH YOU. AND DO NOT WORRY THAT YOUR LIFE IS TURNING UPSIDE DOWN. HOW DO YOU KNOW THAT THE SIDE YOU ARE

USED TO IS BETTER THAN THE ONE TO COME?"

I was not reading the full novel page by page because I liked reading these rules, so I ended up opening the pages with the "rules" written in the novel.

I checked my watch and rushed to the class to attend the lecture.

There was something different about "Creative Writing" classes. Maybe because I love writing, I love attending my classes. I kept thinking about Cooper, his touch, and his smell. Whatever I do, I can't stop thinking about him, even for a second. He had hypnotized my mind and my body.

Next morning, when I woke up, I saw my mom's message, "Landed Safely."

I rushed out of bed, took a shower, and asked Mary to make breakfast ready for all of us. I checked my phone again to see if Cooper had messaged and told myself that maybe he is busy that's why he didn't message me. I always wanted him to message me first. Even if I miss him madly, I want him to tell me that he misses me.

I went down to pick up my parents. I loved seeing them, although I was still thinking about him.

"What's up with my baby? You look weak" my mother said.

"I missed you both a lot," I said.

Mary was delighted to see them more than me. We had breakfast together after a long time.

"Coffee tastes amazing, Mary" Mom said.

The delighted eyes of Mary said 'THANK YOU' even without saying it.

"Have your parents reached"? My phone buzzed.

A sense of calm ran through my body when I saw his text on my phone, and I replied, "Yes, they are here."

The best part of my parent's visit was the gifts. I was showered with clothes, perfumes, and makeup. That was my favorite part of the whole trip. Shopping together and eating out at fancy restaurants was another. My parents were tired, so they went to bed early, and I told my mom about the Chocolab café and the amazing coffee they serve.

We planned to visit the next day because I wanted her to meet Cooper soon.

I came to my bed. I missed Cooper. He was everywhere. He was with me in the room. He was with me on the bed, and when I looked out the window, I felt like my head was on his arms. He was in my every breath. He was in my mind every damn second. I kept tossing in bed and kept missing him like crazy. I checked my phone to see his message and wanted him to text, 'I miss you'. Instead, I chose to wait for his text. I got up and pulled out my diary. Writing is my favorite therapy, by far. The calmness in my soul I get after writing is unexplainable. It's one of the best things one can do.

5th January

I miss you, Cooper. I miss you so fucking much. I wish I could tear my heart open and show how crazily I miss you right now. Do you miss me like I do? Do you even think of me when you are with your friends? Do you wait for my message like I do? I want to text you and talk to you, but I am still not sure whether you would like to talk to me or not. Call me, please, and tell me you miss me. Message me and tell me you missed me sitting next to you in your car while driving.

I put the diary back in the drawer and looked at my phone again.

I sighed sadly and slept.

Chapter-8

I woke up early the next morning, around 8 a.m. to go to the university. I put on my new dress, which my mom bought for me, and texted Leila to pick me up on the way.

"Pick me up, babes. I am ready."

"Sure, at your door in 10 minutes, finishing my breakfast."

I went down to the gate to wait for Leila and texted my mom that I had left for college, but I didn't wake her up because she was tired and sleeping.

"See you, Maa. Leila came to pick me up. Enjoy your time with dear Mary"—I sent her a text with a wink emoji.

Leila honked towards me, and I waved a "HI" and went to her car.

"Mom and dad arrived last night."

"Wow, that's wonderful. I will come to meet them. Let me know when you guys have time"- she answered.

I was only thinking of seeing Cooper tonight. I was also sad that he hadn't messaged me since last night. He didn't hear me say, I miss you, Cooper. Message me, please.

Zero telepathy between me and him. I thought.

I attended my writing class, where I got the prompt to write a LinkedIn ad. I made the ad, sent it to my professor, and rushed out of the class to the school café. Cooper did not message me in one hour and I felt like I don't like this world. I don't like anyone. I hate everyone I see, and this time the whole night passed and half morning he still didn't send any text. I started to panic, and my one leg started shaking in stress. I decided to message him. I didn't want to ask him, how are you? And, where are you? I didn't want to show him that I was under some stupid stress just because he didn't message me. I didn't want to tell him that even if you are busy with your work, family, or friends, send me a text every 15 minutes just to tell me you miss me. Because I miss you, Cooper, what did you do to me? A tear rolled down my eye. How can someone start to affect you so much? I'm going crazy for him, but he doesn't seem to care.

I picked up my phone and texted him, "I will bring my mom to your café. Ask your chef to make the best coffee for her."

"That sounds amazing. See you at 9"- he replied back.

I felt good to see his text. It's so weird to see that one message from him can make me so happy and stress free.

Why has my whole life started to revolve around him? Why am I getting so emotionally attached to him? What if we will not be together in the future?? How am I going to live without him? I had too many questions in my mind and only one answer – I LOVE COOPER. I can't think beyond this. I just know if he ever leaves me or cheats on me, I will be finished. I will die.

He changed me so much. I was a very outgoing and friendly person. I was the funniest in my friend group and in my family. Everyone loved to be around me. But now I only want to meet him every day and every night. I don't want to meet my other friends. I don't want to go out with Leila. I cancel my plans if any friend asks me to meet. I only want to spend every single second of my time with Cooper. I want to be around him all the time. My social life has become zero. Only his presence makes me happy. Only his messages made me relax.

I went home after my class. My university was 25 minutes away from where I lived. I called my sister to talk and to tell her that I miss her more now that our parents are here. We talked for 20 minutes about every detail, from what my mom brought for me to what we were going to eat for lunch today.

I saw Mary near the lift in my building with lots of juices and soft drinks. My father always filled my fridge with my favorite drinks.

"Come, sweetie, lunch is ready"—my mom hugged me when she saw me on the door.

I needed that hug, I felt.

I loved seeing my parents when I came back. At least I saw someone else other than Mary.

We had lunch together. Mom took charge of cooking my favorite pasta and gave Mary a rest today.

"We will go to the café around 9, mom".

"Sure, sweetie, I will be ready," she said.

"You too, join us" My mother asked Dad.

"You guys go ahead and have your girls time. I will be at home watching a movie tonight," he answered.

I thought about Cooper. I thought about him in my home with me and my parents eating lunch together.

Chapter-9

I told my mom to get ready and told Mary to give dinner to my dad.

I took my old pair of Guess jeans and my MK blue sweater, which my mom bought this time. I was super excited for my mom to meet Cooper, though I didn't tell her that she would meet a friend of mine in the café.

We reached the café exactly at 9 p.m. I looked at my mom's face, and she looked content with my choice, and I felt relieved. We grabbed my usual table near the stairs and scanned the whole café to look for Cooper. He was not there.

"Maybe he is inside," I said to myself.

We ordered pizza, mushroom ravioli, and café lattes for both of us.

"This place is pretty. Kind of different than other cafes", mom said.

"Yes, totally. The ambience is different, and the staff is friendlier"- I said.

I want mom to like this café as much as I like this place. I waited for Cooper. I texted him.

"Where are you? I am here."

"I am just parking the car. Come into the parking lot. I want to talk to you," he replied.

"How can I come?" My mom is here.

"Make an excuse. It's urgent. Please come."

I told my mom that we didn't pay the full amount to the cab driver, and now he texted me that I need to pay more, so I will go to the parking area to pay him the rest of the amount.

"Do you want me to come with you?" mom said.

"It's okay. I will go and come back fast. You wait here."- I told her.

I went to the parking lot and moved towards his car. It was right there, near the stairs, like always. He opened the door of the car, and I sat inside.

"Hey, tell me what is so urgent?" I asked.

"I want to kiss you. It's been days since I kissed you."

"Did you miss me?" I asked.

"Yes, a lot" he replied.

"Kiss me." I said.

He removed his seat belt, held my face in his warm hands, and kissed me on the cheeks. One by one on both sides. I closed my eyes and felt his lips touching my skin. He then pressed his lips softly against mine. I moved my hands inside his hair to the back of his nape.

He sucked my mouth as if he was starving, and I loved him sucking my mouth to feel that he was starving for me. He opened his eyes, looked into mine, and said, "Give me your tongue." I put my tongue gently in his mouth and closed my eyes again to feel him sucking it. He gently pulled my tongue into his mouth and sucked it. He gently bit my lower lip, and I madly kissed his lips.

"I missed you," I said while kissing his mouth.

He kissed me more, again and again, harder, as if he missed me more than I missed him.

"Let's go, Cooper, I said."

He looked into my eyes and said, Let's go home.

I laughed and said, Sure, next time, but right now, mom is waiting. She must be wondering where I went for so long.

"First, I will go. Come after 5 minutes," I said.

I tied up my hair again and looked into the mirror to see if I looked fine after this hot car kissing session.

I went up to the café to my table loaded with dinner and coffee.

"Why did it take so much time?" mom asked.

"His card machine was not working," I said.

"Anyway, let's eat." I said.

As soon as I stuffed my mouth with pizza, I saw Cooper's WhatsApp on my phone.

"I wish I was that pizza in your mouth."

I looked around. He was standing right in front of me, but a few tables away.

He winked at me, and I tried not to smile because of my mom.

"It was so cheesy, Cooper" I replied back.

After we finished our meal, I saw Cooper coming towards my table.

"Hey, long time, Serah. How have you been?" He said that and offered his hand for a shake.

"Hey, been busy with university"- I said.

"Meet my mom"—I pointed towards my mom.

"Mom, this is Cooper. He owns this café." I introduced Cooper to her.

They both shook hands and smiled.

"Nice café, Cooper" mom said.

"Thanks, Miss", enjoy your time." Cooper replied.

"Let me know if you need anything" he said to me.

"Oh, thanks much, but we are about to leave" I said.

We both smiled and waved goodbye to each other.

We booked a cab and left for home.

"He seems to be a nice guy," mom said.

"Yes, he is." I answered.

I felt happy to see mom liking Cooper instantly. He was like this. Always smiling with his bright eyes and gorgeous smile. Always throwing positive vibes. I loved his aura. The positivity and charm he carried were the most attractive parts. Me being the funny one, we always kept laughing with each other on silly jokes we cracked together.

"Have you guys reached? It was lovely meeting your mom." He messaged.

"Yes, we have reached five minutes back, she liked meeting you too," I replied.

"When am I going to see you again?" he messaged back.

He wants to see me again. I smiled.

"No idea. Maybe after tomorrow when they will go back"- I replied.

"Okay, I am going to miss you" he said.

"I will miss you too" I replied.

I think I will have a very good sleep tonight for two reasons. First, we kissed in his car. Second, he said he would miss me. I took out my diary and mentioned the date.

8th January

I loved kissing Cooper. I loved how he messaged me to meet him in his car. I found it so romantic. I loved his taste, his lips, and his smell. I wish he could kiss me every single day for the rest of our lives. I love Cooper so much that sometimes I feel sad about myself. I wonder if he could ever love me back like I do. I knew somewhere in my heart that if he ever left me, I would be ruined. This love will ruin me because, in this relationship, I am the one who is vulnerable. I am the one who loves more.

I finished writing and put the diary back.

I pulled over the blanket on my face and thought, Are we even in a relationship? He didn't propose to me, and he didn't ask me to be his girlfriend. What kind of relationship do I have with him? I should talk to Cooper and know his intentions and what he thinks about me. I will meet him the day after tomorrow.

Chapter-10

We went shopping the next morning. My mom has to buy useless stuff for her kitchen and for herself. I kept thinking about what to say to him and where to meet.

"Where are you lost today?" mom asked me.

"umm, Nowhere. I'm just wondering if you would meet Leila for dinner or not." I said.

"I love that girl. I brought her a nice dress. Sure, I will see her."

Sure, I will message her and let her know that we will meet for dinner. We decided to meet Leila at a Persian restaurant. My mom loves kebabs, so Leila invited us to a Persian restaurant and told me that she would pick us up sharp at 8 p.m.

So, we went for dinner, and mom loved the food. The kebabs are scrumptious and succulent. They served it with saffron rice and a dash of butter, with juicy kebabs on the sides. My parents were leaving next morning, and me being the most selfish, I cannot wait for them to go because I have to talk to Cooper about our relationship status.

My parents flight was early in the morning the next day, and I decided to meet Cooper the same day. I didn't have my college because of Sunday, so I told him to meet at 11 a.m.

"I want to meet you tomorrow at 11 a.m. if you are free," I texted him.

"Yes, I am free. Where would you like to meet?"

"Come my home" I said.

"Okay, see you tomorrow" he replied.

Mom and dad left early in the morning, around 7 a.m., and I slept again for a few hours.

I woke up again around 10 and told Mary to go to the bank because she wanted to send money to her family. I told her to message me before coming back, as today is Sunday and I might go out with friends. Mary left around 10.30, and I changed into my normal pajamas and tee shirt. I didn't want to change into something good or look good for him. If he wanted to be with me, he would choose me in this appearance.

He came exactly at 11 a.m. and texted me to ask about my flat number.

I replied back to him and waited for the bell to ring soon. As the bell rang, I felt so nervous, as it was his first time in my home. My home is not as pretty as his because I am still a student, but he is a well-established businessman, so he has a proper, beautiful setup in his home.

I went to the door and opened the gate.

"Hey." he hugged me, and I hugged him back.

"I baked this lotus biscoff cheesecake for you. I hope you like it"—he handed me a pretty cake platter.

'Oh! Thank you so much.' I opened the platter. The cake looks mouth-watering. I said.

I kept it in the kitchen and asked him to sit on the sofa.

I brought two slices of cake and took a bite from my plate.

"Oh my god, Cooper, this is the yummiest lotus cheesecake I ever tasted. You are so talented, and I am so lucky that you baked it for me."

"Thank you, sweetheart. Next time, I will bake cookies for you," Cooper said.

"Aww, that's so kind of you! If you keep feeding me like this, I will put on weight very fast." I replied.

We both laughed and took another bite of the cake.

"So, what you wanted to talk to me, Serah?" Cooper questioned.

I thought for a while, then said, "What am I to you? We kissed a few times, and we had sex, but it's still not clear what you think of me?"

"Cooper held my hand and said, I love you, Serah. I have never felt this kind of love before. I think about you all the time. I think about seeing you all the time. I think of kissing you all the time." He leaned forward and kissed my cheek.

"I love you too, Cooper. I love you more than anything in this world. I love you more than my life. I loved you the moment I saw you for the first time. I prayed to see you every time until I came to know that café is yours. I used to come to the café just to see you. I love you madly."

"Cooper hugged me so tightly as if all of my burden washed away."

"So, I am your girlfriend"—I asked again because I wanted the assurance again.

"Yes, I am your boyfriend, and you are my girlfriend. And we are dating each other. He smiled and gave me the assurance I wanted."

"I was never happier than I feel right now," I told him.

"Do you know what I love about you the most?" Cooper asked.

"Nope" I said.

"You are not like other girls. You never cared to impress me with your looks, your attire, or your appearance. It was the most attractive thing to me. There are girls out there who would do anything or change themselves for my attention, but you never did that. You never cared to wear sexy clothes to grab my attention. Even today you are in your pajamas" he laughed.

That baggy pair of pants and boyfriend t-shirt took my heart away. Your beauty is in your simplicity.

I pulled him down on the carpet from the sofa and sat on his lap, facing him.

"I love to sit near your face like this," I said.

"I love it when your face is this close to mine"- he replied.

I rubbed his lower lip gently with my thumb, and he grabbed my thumb in his mouth and sucked it. I looked into his eyes and smiled. He held me by my back and pushed me more into him. He kissed my lips. I kissed him back. He kissed me more, and I kissed him more.

He took his hand under my t-shirt and grabbed my breast with both of his hands.

I moaned softly into his mouth and sucked his lips hard. I pushed my mouth more into his mouth and rubbed my tongue with his. His mouth felt warm, and his mouth smelled nice. I didn't want to stop kissing him.

"I want to eat you," he said.

"Eat me, please" I replied.

I held his hand, moved it into my pajamas, and moaned softly when his warm fingers touched my pussy.

I removed his shirt and ran my fingers on his neck rather than his shoulder.

I removed my shirt, then my bra, and hugged him. The warmth of his body was exploding my senses. Our bodies touched like magnets, and I didn't want him to get away from mine.

Cooper took one cushion from the sofa, kept it on the carpet, and pushed me on it. My head was on the cushion, and he was sitting near my legs.

He removed my pajamas and opened my legs a bit with his hands. He put his mouth on my pussy over my panty and breathed hard on it.

"Oh god, Cooper, I feel your breath down"- I said.

"Yeah, baby"- he said.

He kissed my inner thighs softly, then pulled my panty from the side and gently touched my clit with the tip of his tongue.

I moaned like crazy.

"Remove my panty" I told him.

He removed my panty and went again between my legs. I saw his face between my legs, spitting on my pussy to make it more wet, and then he softly started eating me out. He rubbed his tongue up and down on my clit. He then opened my pussy lips with his fingers and softly put the tip of his tongue inside my vaginal opening. I pulled his hair into pleasure and pushed his face more into my vagina. I was groaning with pleasure.

"Oh, Cooper, I love you."

He came up to my mouth and sucked my mouth. "I love you too."

"Fuck me" I said.

"I don't have condoms," he replied.

"Put your fingers inside. Just finger-fuck me. I need you inside me" I said.

He put his two fingers into my mouth, and I sucked them really hard until they were dripping wet. He then put his fingers inside my vagina, and I bit his side of the neck out of pleasure. He started to move his fingers in and out slowly, then harder and harder. He rubbed my clitoris with his fingers harder and harder, and I kissed his mouth and kept on kissing him until I came on his fingers.

We hugged each other and stayed in each other's arms until Cooper's phone started ringing.

I saw the name on the screen—Miss Donat.

He didn't pick up the call, and the same name started calling again and again, three to four times.

I asked him, who is calling you on Sunday?

"It's someone from work," he said.

"But you work alone"- I replied.

Cooper thought for a while and said, it's someone from the past, and I don't care about her.

I got up, put on my shirt and trousers without saying a word, and asked Cooper to leave.

"Please try to understand. It's nothing between me and her. I don't know why she is calling," he said.

"Cooper, leave" I said.

"Please don't ruin this moment. Hear me out"- he answered.

"I don't want to hear anything. Just leave."

He left, and I went straight to my bed and started crying a lot.

10th January

I took out my diary and started pouring out my feelings on paper. Is he cheating on me? Why did he never mention his ex? Why is she calling him now? Is he double-dating both of us? Oh God, no. Is Cooper a playboy? I just had sex with him, and the Ex called. Maybe he has to meet her? I want answers, Cooper. I hate you, dammit.

I finished writing, switched off my phone, and went to sleep.

When everything goes wrong and you don't know what to do next—switch off your phone and go to sleep.

Chapter-11

I woke up the next day with a heavy heart and a lot of hate for everyone and everything and saw Cooper's missed calls and a few WhatsApp messages about how it was a misunderstanding, and I took it wrong. He called again as soon as I woke up and asked to meet me. But I overcame my anger, and I agreed to meet him as if seeing his face would wipe off my anger and sadness. We decided to meet each other at Chocolab Café at 12 p.m. for lunch. I didn't want to get ready. I felt my heart broken. I changed my clothes and waited for the clock to tick at 12 p.m. I only wanted to hear his part. I only wanted him to tell me the truth. I only wanted him to assure me that he would never cheat on me.

I reached the café exactly at 12, and I saw Cooper waiting for me.

"Hey," he said.

"Hey," I said.

I didn't hug him. I didn't want to. I can't be physically attached to someone until my heart and mind are clear about them. I even hate physical touch if I have grudges against someone. And Cooper was the first guy who got so close to me, so I hated him more at that moment, as much as I didn't want to look up at his face.

"How are you?" he asked me.

"I am fine," I mumbled.

Tell me why you wanted to meet me. I said

"Why are you in a hurry?" He smiled and asked.

"Are you crazy?" I said. You are smiling. What's so funny about this moment?

He laughed upon hearing this, which made me furious. I didn't say a word after that and waited for him to clear his part.

"Look, Serah, I had something with her in the past that was not serious at all."

"Who is she?" I asked.

"Someone from the café" he said.

"WHO?" I asked with curiosity.

"A waitress, she needed money, so I helped her a few times."

"Oh my God, you dated a waitress"— I was shocked to know this.

"I never met her outside café"- he said.

"It's not possible that you dated someone and you didn't meet her outside," I mumbled.

"You should know that I don't love her. I never did. I never met her outside of this café. I only helped her for money." She left this café and works somewhere else now.

"Then why is she calling you now?" I asked.

"I don't know. She calls sometimes and sends me messages, but I never pick up her call or reply to her"- he said.

"I love you only. I never loved anyone like I loved you," he said.

"Yeah, sure"- I replied.

"Forget about her, please. It's nothing," he said.

"So why don't you block her?" I asked.

"I will block her," he said.

Cooper couldn't make me feel fine or clear my doubts. If he doesn't have anything with her and if she calls him every now and then, then why didn't Cooper block her? I still had questions in my mind. Maybe he likes attention. Maybe he likes it when girls message or call him. Maybe he still talks to her, that's why she called. Too many questions were piled up in my mind, but I didn't talk to Cooper about him because I don't know if he is telling me the truth or making it all up. Maybe it was a bit too early to fall in love with him. What if I made the mistake of falling in love with him?

"Dear Serah, be ready to get your heart broken again and again. It's just the first time. Wait and see what else he has in his past or present. He is going to hurt you a lot,"- I told myself.

"I want to go back home"- I told him.

"I will drop you" he said.

"No thanks. I have booked the cab already."

I said bye to him, went to the parking area of the cab, and went home.

On my way back home, I kept thinking about Cooper and how he didn't care to clear my doubts. He took it so lightly that he was laughing at seeing me angry. He didn't answer any of my questions except by telling me, "I love you. I don't love her."

I wanted more than this. Women need proper clarification for the things that hurt them, but Cooper was very normal, as if being in touch with an ex is a normal thing when you are already committed to another person. I felt like he doesn't care about my feelings. He didn't care to uplift my mood.

Maybe I am too devoted to him, or maybe I got into a relationship with him a bit early.

I reached home, paid the driver, took the lift to my floor, and went straight to bed.

My phone rang. It was his message.

"I love you. Please don't think anything wrong."

"It's okay" I replied.

He didn't reply back.

Chapter-12

I didn't go to college the next day. When I am upset or angry with Cooper, I don't want to do anything. I don't know why it affects me so much that I leave my classes, my food, and everything. I miss him. I want him to message me and ask me to meet him. I want him to message me and ask me how I am doing today. I want him to ask me if I am still upset.

He doesn't give me as much importance as I give him. I made him the center of my world, but his world revolves around too many people, and I am the last one he thinks about.

I've spent the entire day in bed. Reading or scrolling my phone, turning and twisting in my bed, only waiting for his call or message because I know his one message will change my mood. If he asks to meet me, I know I will say "yes." That's how weak I am when it comes to Cooper. I have lost my self-respect, and I know it, but I feel I love Cooper above everything, and this makes me very sad sometimes that the love I give to him doesn't get back in return.

I saw my phone. It was 5 p.m. I woke up and made some tea for myself when I saw my phone ringing. It was Cooper. I didn't pick. He called again. I didn't pick for the second time either. I finished my tea and went to sit in my lounge. My mind was occupied with Cooper and his ex-girlfriend. He called again, and I picked up.

"Hey"- I said.

"Hey, how are you?" he asked.

"I am fine, you?"

"I am good. I want to see you"- he said.

"Okay, come home" I said.

"Alright, see you at 10 p.m." He replied, cutting the phone.

I was not happy at all. My heart is broken, and I know only he can fix it by just telling me he loves me. I hate myself for giving him so much opportunity and for being so helpless that even his little effort will make me happy.

I got sadder by thinking this, then I told myself, "There is nothing special about Cooper. He can't even love me properly, and he can't make little efforts to make me happy. He is a very cold person when it comes to love. What makes him special is my love. My unconditional love makes him special. My care and attention make him special. My weakness of heart for him makes him special. Cooper is not special. My love is special. It is me who is special. It is me who is loving someone as cold as him. It's my special love that makes him special."

I don't know why he wants to see me, but I started waiting for him.

My phone rang, and it was his message: Do you need something?

"I need you, Cooper, an honest and loving Cooper" I thought.

"No, nothing. Thank you," I replied.

After half an hour, my doorbell rang, and it was him at the door. There was one thing good about Mary. She never used to come out of her room when Leila or Cooper visited me at night. She still didn't see Cooper, even though he has visited my home quite a few times now.

I went to get him and opened the door. There he was smiling in his yellow t-shirt and black jeans—that bright and charming smile that transfers me to an enchanted world and makes me tender and weak in my bones.

"Hey" he said and hugged me.

I hugged him back, and he came inside to sit on the couch.

"So, how are you?" He asked me.

"I am fine" I said without looking at his face.

He knew I was still upset, but he ignored my request to ask me instead, saying, you look pretty.

"More than your ex-girlfriend?" I asked.

He smiled and said, I don't remember her anymore.

"Asshole" I said to him.

"He laughed and pulled my cheek with his hand."

"I love you. I have never loved anybody like I love you. Please trust me."

"I love you too" I smiled and hugged him.

He smells wonderful. I love his smell.

"You smell so nice", he said surprisingly.

"Can I smell your neck?" he asked.

I pulled my hair away from my neck and said, "Yes."

He rubbed the tip of his nose on my neck softly and took a warm breath on it, sending me shivers down to my spine.

I took my hands in his hair and grasped his mouth against my lips.

"Let's go to your bedroom," he said.

I held his hand to get up and walked towards my room. I pushed him against the wall and kissed his mouth until I stopped breathing. I love his mouth, his lips, his scent, and his skin. I love everything about Cooper. He makes love to me as if he never made love to anybody. I feel safe when he kisses me, but his actions confuse me.

He took his hands inside my shirt, and I unbuttoned his shirt while kissing him. I took him towards the bed and pushed him onto the bed. His eyes traced my body while I removed my shirt and sat on his thighs. I held his hands and kept them on my breasts, pressing them gently with his hand.

"Oh Serah" he moaned my name while rubbing his forefinger on my nipples.

"I love you, Cooper," I said in his ear, and he held me as tightly as he could, wrapping his hands around my waist.

"I want to lie down in bed with you," I said.

He hugged me and pulled the blankets on us. I slept in his arms until 6 a.m. His alarm rang. He checked his phone, put on his clothes, hugged me, and left.

I am glad he left before Mary woke up. I slept a little more, hugging myself and wearing his scent on my body. I don't want to take a shower after sex with Cooper because I love his scent on my body, on my pillow, and in my blanket. I wanted to stay in bed all day, but Leila called exactly at 8 a.m. to check on me.

"Do you want to attend class today?" she asked me.

"Yes, pick me up in half an hour," I replied.

I felt happy this morning because Cooper was with me the whole night, though the face that his Ex still calls him made me sad again, and I flicked the thought by thinking about the love he made for me last night.

The weather is quite cold in February, so I took my overcoat and boots and left for university.

"You are not regular to college these days. What's up with you?" Leila asked.

"Um, nothing. I just don't feel like attending university. Feeling a bit lazy these days."

"Sure, the examiner will also be too lazy to give you marks in exams" Leila winked, and we both laughed.

"I miss you. I loved that you stayed with me last night"- I texted Cooper.

"I miss you too. I loved sleeping with you. It was so peaceful. I had a very good sleep"- he replied back.

I smiled and went to my class.

The professor gave us the prompt, "If you could be in charge of the world for one day, what would you do?"

I started writing on my laptop, but the thought of Cooper and the night we spent together in bed kept messing with my head, so I finished the assignment before everyone else and left the class. Cooper took over my senses, and I am not good for anything anymore. I can't do anything. I can't work. I can't focus on my studies. I can't sleep or eat. He is everywhere inside me.

He is breathing in me. He exists in my body and brain all the time. I don't know when and how I lost myself that I feel like I am not me anymore.

"I know an amazing place for burgers, let's go tonight"- Cooper messaged.

"Whoa, I love burgers. Let's go," I replied.

I went back to my home, had lunch, and took a nice nap in the same bed where Cooper hugged me and slept, with the same bedsheet, the same blanket, and the same pillow. I wore my new black cargo pants and new orange hoodie, got ready, and waited for Cooper to come and pick me up. I always get so excited to see him, as if I am seeing him for the first time. My love for him is dangerous. If he ever leaves me or cheats on me, I will be damaged, ruined, and destroyed.

My thoughts went to puddles when Cooper called and told me to come down in the next 5 minutes.

I hurried up, took my purse, and went down.

"You look gorgeous" I hugged and told him.

"Thank you, baby, not more than you" he answered.

We soon reached a cute little burger joint. They had an open sitting area with small wooden benches and a wooden table. The area was a bit small, and it had three to four benches. People prefer to order from drive-thru in this season, although Cooper and I parked the car and went to take our table.

"One crispy chicken burger for me"- I told the waiter.

"Beef burger for me with jalapenos and two cokes." Cooper ordered.

Cooper took a few pictures of me, and I kind of find it cute to click my pictures without telling me. He sent me the pictures on WhatsApp, and I checked and told him, "You can never click a single good picture of mine." He laughed.

Our order came, and we enjoyed the burger and coke in this windy weather.

The crispy chicken patty melted in the mouth, and the burger was finger-licking good.

"I don't like jalapenos"- I told Cooper.

"Oh, I love jalapenos," he replied.

"Yes, I can see that" I answered.

We walked down to the parking lot, and Cooper drove me off to my home.

He always held my hand while driving, and I always loved it more than anything when he asked for my hand. Whenever he drives his car, I wait for him to ask for my hand to hold it. And he always does. Even if it's a small drive from café to home. The most romantic part is, he never leaves my hand while changing the gear of car or while parking the car. He always uses one hand to change the gear and to hold the steering and hold my hand with another hand.

I love small, silly things about Cooper.

He dropped me back home, kissed me good night, and went to his home.

"I really had a fun-tastic night with you. I love you" I messaged him.

"Me too, my love. Take care and sleep well"- he replied.

"Tomorrow is Valentine's day and I want to spend whole evening with you"- I messaged him.

"Done babe"- he answered.

I couldn't wait for the next day to meet Cooper. This was my first Valentine's with someone I love. I never felt the importance of Valentine's Day until I met Cooper.

I got a text from him saying that he would meet me at 7 p.m. and we would go out. I was excited to step out in the city with him as his Valentine. I changed my outfit and wore a full black dress, put on a bit of makeup, and waited for him to pick me up.

Cooper called me exactly at 7 p.m. One thing that I love about him is that he is always on time, no matter what.

I took the gift I bought for Cooper and went down to the parking lot, where he was waiting for me. Every time I see his car, my heart skips a beat. I am crazily in love with Cooper. I feel it in my bones. I feel it everywhere in my body—in every nerve, in every heartbeat, and in every breath, I take.

I opened the door of his car and sat inside.

"Hey" I said, giving my big smile.

"Hey, how are you?" He asked, smiling back at me.

I hugged him, and he hugged me back.

"I am fine. How are you?" I asked.

"You look handsome, and I am fine," I said.

There is one thing about myself of which I am really proud. I love complimenting people. I love telling them that they look great, that they have a good smile, or that I like their clothes. I love telling Cooper that I find him handsome. My love for him is so intense that I tell him every now and then how handsome he is. How amazing he cooks or bakes. I love complimenting him. I love making him feel good about himself. I wanted him to know that I appreciated him and love everything about him. I love making other people happy about themselves. I love supporting people and encouraging them.

We went to a nice café somewhere 30 minutes away from my home. The café was full of couples because of Valentine's Day. We took our seats and ordered our food.

"I got something for you," Cooper said, handing me a cute little carry bag of red color.

I opened the carry bag, which had a small box packed with red ribbon. I opened the ribbon and box.

"Oh my god, that's lovely, Cooper. I loved it. It's beautiful"- I said happily while looking at the beautiful red-colored heart-shaped pendent with a silver-colored chain in it.

I wore it in my hand as a bracelet because of my turtle-neck dress, and I don't like wearing jewelry on turtle neck dresses. It was radiating on my wrist, and I loved wearing it because of its importance, as Cooper gifted me.

"I love you so much, Cooper"- I said, looking at my cute little pendant cum bracelet.

"I love you too, baby" Cooper answered.

"This is for you. I hope you like it." I gifted Cooper my favorite Christian Dior 'poison' perfume.

He opened the box, sprayed it on his wrist, and smelled it.

"It smells lovely. Thank you so much, baby," he said.

"Thank you, Cooper. I loved the gift." I said again, looking at my cute little heart-shaped pendant, which I wore on my wrist as a bracelet.

I looked at my watch, and it was already 12 a.m. We spent three hours together, and it felt like three minutes. Time always flew quite fast when I am with Cooper, and I hated it about time. A three-hour meeting felt like a three-minute meet-up.

I love him so much. I told myself while looking at him. He was busy using his phone, and I was busy looking at his face. I never bothered about the hundreds of people around me whenever I was with Cooper. I only looked at him. Everything and everyone around me were just background music. I always felt like he was the only person in the room, in spite of the thousands of people around. I never bothered to look around. I never took my eyes off him whenever he was with me. I felt happy looking at him. I felt happy that I found him, but it always scares me a lot to love him like this. It always scared me to fall in love with him so intensely. I tell myself more than a thousand times a day that "I love Cooper" even when I am with him. Every now and then, I find myself saying, "I love him madly. What should I do with this much love that I feel for him?"

Cooper looked up at my face and questioned, "What are you thinking?"

"I just love you so much. I hope that you never break my heart"- I said.

"I love you too, and I will never break your heart"- he replied.

He dropped me home and kissed me good night.

"Good night, baby."

"Good night, Cooper"- I said.

Chapter-13

I woke up the next morning with a smile on my face. I kept thinking about the cute gift that Cooper gave me. I still had it on my wrist.

Mary made me a hot cup of tea. I took the cup from the table and sat on my sofa. I kept looking at my wrist and thinking about how much I loved him. For once, I thought, why is it that I always think about how much I love Cooper but never about how much Cooper loves me?

The smile on my face faded away.

Is Cooper playing with me? Is he dating another woman also? Is he faking his love? Is he with me because I make him feel good about himself? Is he with me because nobody has ever loved him so much? These questions burned in my head, and I suddenly started losing my senses.

Then I told myself about everything he did for me.

He meets me even when he is occupied with work. He took me out on Valentine's Day. He cares for me when I am angry.

I thought about good things and felt fine.

I picked up my phone and texted him, "Hey, where are you? I miss you."

"Hey baby, I miss you too. Come home tonight. We will watch a movie"- he replied.

"Okay, see you." I answered.

I lay down on my sofa and felt low. I had this feeling of loneliness and sadness that engulfed my heart, and I felt the tears rolling down my cheek in the next few minutes.

I always have this fear that Cooper will leave me or that he will find another woman better than me. Sometimes I felt as if he doesn't love me like I love him. He doesn't express as much love as I do. But one thing I am sure of is that nobody will love him like I do. I prayed to God that he would never break my heart, or else I would go crazy.

I cried so much, as if he had left me already or cheated on me. I wish he could see my sadness, hear me crying, and assure me that he will never leave me. He will be with me always, and he will only love me forever.

I got up. I went to my room, took my clothes, and went to take a shower.

I ordered our favorite cold Spanish latte and sat in my bathtub full of hot water for a few minutes to relax my mind and calm my body.

I saw the mobile, and it was already 8.30. I took a shower and came out.

I dried my hair while waiting for the latte to arrive.

I booked the cab as soon as my latte arrived and went down to the parking lot to wait for the cab.

The whole time I was in the cab, I kept thinking, "Does he love me truly, honestly, or he just enjoys my company?"

"Why suddenly did I feel so many emotions as if something had happened?"

I arrived at his home, paid the driver, and went inside his apartment.

Cooper looked dapper in his loose-fitting black t-shirt and grey trouser. I love his care free look when he is at home. He looks more attractive when he is by himself at home in his comfort zone.

I hugged him and sat down on his sofa while he was in the kitchen, getting me a doughnut, he had baked.

"Here it is. Try and let me know." He said he was giving me the plate of doughnuts.

I took the first bite of the chocolate-laden doughnut— "it's amazing Cooper, so yummy" I said.

"Thank you," he said with a wide grin on his face.

He sat close to me on the sofa, covering my shoulders with his arm. I laid my head on his arm and he kissed on my forehead.

I closed my eyes, and he kissed me on my eyes, then on my cheek. I felt his warm lips on my skin. He touched my lips with his. I kissed him back while still resting my head on his arm.

"I love the taste of the doughnut now" he said while kissing me.

I smiled and closed my eyes again.

His phone rang, and I saw the text, "Hey, are you there?"

He saved the name with the letter 'M'.

"Who is 'M' Cooper?" I asked him.

He looked nervous.

"My cousin" he replied.

"Why would you save your cousin's number as 'M'?" I asked.

He looked at my face, and I saw his face turning pale.

I was anxious. I asked him again.

"What's your cousin's real name?"

He stayed silent.

I held his face in my hands. "I love you, Cooper. Please tell me the truth."

"I love you too, Serah", he replied.

"Who is that?" I asked again.

"It is only a friend from Café" he replied.

"What's her name? Why didn't you save her name?" I asked.

"I don't know, but she is just a friend. I swear" he replied.

"How did she find your number?" I asked him.

"She airdropped me her Snapchat ID, and I accepted" he replied.

"And what does she want from you at 1 a.m. at night?"—I asked with tears in my eyes.

"I don't know Serah"—he answered the same thing again.

"For how long are you talking to her?" I asked.

"Since last month" he answered.

Tears rolled down from my eyes, and I couldn't speak a single word.

"I swear there is nothing between me and her. I love you only" he hugged me and said.

"Please don't cry" she is just a normal friend. He said it again.

"What's her name?" I asked.

"Josephine" he replied.

"I promise I will block her right now. Don't be sad," he said.

I didn't say anything.

"He showed me that he blocked her from Snapchat and WhatsApp."

"Okay, I need to go home" I said.

"It's late. Go in the morning" he said.

I want to go now. I will book a cab. I said.

"Don't book a cab, I will drop you" he said.

I got up from the sofa, took my jacket, and went to the parking lot.

There was silence between us. I didn't speak, and he didn't say a word.

He stopped the car.

I said goodnight to him and went to my flat.

I lied down on my bed and comforted myself—"he blocked her."

"Why would he save her number as 'M'? Why would she message him at 1 at night?"

"She is just a friend. He wouldn't have blocked her if there was something else. I have to trust Cooper"- I told myself.

My phone rang, and I saw Cooper's message.

"Hey Serah, I am sorry I made you sad. Trust me, I love you only. I am sorry I can't express my love like you do, but I only love you, and I have never loved anybody else like this."

"I trust you" I replied back.

I switched off my phone and went to sleep.

I woke up the next day around 10 a.m. I missed my class.

I turned my phone on and saw four missed calls from Cooper.

"Hey, I was sleeping" I didn't call him. Instead, I sent him a message.

"Hey, I want to meet you" he replied.

I wanted to tell him I don't want to meet him, but I only wanted to see him. He was the only person in the world who could break my heart and fix it again. I knew I was the weakest person when it came to Cooper.

Even though I was hurt from last night, I still wanted to see him.

Cooper is the only person who can break me and fix me at the same time.

"Okay, I am free" I replied.

"Come to the café" he replied.

"Okay"- I replied.

I got up. I took a shower, got dressed, and booked a cab.

I reached the café and found Cooper sitting there already.

"Hey!" he hugged me.

"Hey!" I said without a smile.

"Show me Josephine." I looked around the café and saw many people, men and women, sitting and enjoying their morning coffee.

"Look at your back, in a white dress," he said.

"I turned back anxiously and with a fear in my heart, thinking what if she was prettier and sexier."

"I looked at her. She was already looking at us as if she knew about me."

She was an older woman, around 45. She maybe a divorced or separated from her husband.

I have seen her almost every day whenever I come to Café. She was always here in the morning as well as at night.

I didn't say anything to Cooper.

"Please be fine" he said.

"I am fine" I said.

We ordered coffee and drank it in silence.

Even though Josephine was sitting exactly in front of Cooper, I didn't mind because Cooper was still sitting with me. I forgave Cooper because I love him madly.

I saw Cooper a few times looking at Josephine, which made me furious.

"What the fuck? Stop looking at her" I said angrily.

"I am not looking at her. She is sitting exactly in front of me. Can't I move my eyes also?" he said.

I was so angry that I didn't say a single word.

"She knows that I love you" Cooper told me.

"Still she is looking at you," I said.

"Please, Serah, trust me. I talked to her normally as a friend," Cooper said.

"The way she is looking at you every now and then doesn't look like she thinks of you as a friend, and I can feel that." I said.

"Forget about her, please. I only love you" he said again.

"Okay" I said.

I came back home around 2 p.m. I couldn't stop thinking about Josephine's eyes on Cooper and Cooper looking back at her.

Oh god, help me. What should I believe? What I saw in the café or what Cooper is telling me. I cried for help from God.

I comforted myself again that Cooper loves me only and that she is just a friend, and she is quite old.

I got up and washed my face. I told myself that Cooper would never break my heart. He knows how much I love him. How madly and crazily I am in love with him. He will never cheat on me.

I played songs on YouTube, read a good book, and waited for his text.

"I will never talk to her again" Cooper texted me.

"I love you, Cooper. Don't break my heart ever" I replied back.

"I am happy with you only, Serah" he messaged again.

"Me too" I replied back.

In the evening, Cooper called and asked me to go out with him for dinner in a new café, which he found recently on Instagram.

He asked me to come out with him. He could have asked another girl or didn't bother to take me out. Instead, he called me and asked me out. I thought.

He told me to get ready by 8 p.m., as he had already made reservations for both of us.

I miss him so much, though I met him in the morning. I miss him so much that I can't wait for the night to see him.

It's amazing and equally painful how much you can love a person. I feel surprised to feel how much love I feel for him. Sometimes it feels like my heart will burst because of the love I have for Cooper. It makes me restless to see how devoted I am to him. I never loved anybody like this before him, and I will never love anyone after him.

It always took me more than an hour to decide what to wear while going out with him. I want to wear the best. I want to look best for him. I want him to look at me and feel lucky to have me like I do. I am head-over heels for him.

I checked my phone and saw two missed calls from Leila.

I called her back.

"Hey, how are you doing?" I asked.

"I am fine, you stranger. Where are you busy these days? Let's catch up tonight" she asked.

"I am a bit busy tonight. Going out with my college friends. Let's meet tomorrow" I said.

"Okay, I will let you know" she said.

"Okay, done"- I said.

Cooper came to pick me up. We hugged each other. He looked handsome as always, and I complimented him as always. "You look hot," I said.

He laughed and said, "Thank you."

He took my hand from my lap and held it in his hand while driving with one hand. I love it when he does that. I always wait for him to hold my hand while driving. Nothing makes me happier than him holding my hand. I feel safe, and I feel loved. I love the power of touch and how calm it can make you.

We reached the café, and it looked quite lavish in its ambience.

"Oh, it's Chinese" I exclaimed.

"Yes, Chinese, because I know you love Chinese" he said.

"Wow, he noticed that I love Chinese cuisine." I thought and smiled.

The café was quite pretty, reflecting the culture and tradition of China.

The wall was covered with traditional Chinese artwork and calligraphy, and Chinese lanterns were hanging down from the roof.

We ordered kung pao chicken, noodles, wontons, and steamed fish.

We waited for our food to arrive. Cooper seemed busy with his phone. He used his phone more than usual, and I almost started thinking about him talking to Josephine. I looked at him for a while. He was so busy that he didn't look up. We didn't talk.

I didn't ask about Josephine, but I realized something was off.

A woman's gut feeling is truer than anything.

"Are you okay?" I asked him.

He looked up at me and said, "Yes, I am fine."

"You look busy" I said.

"No, no. Just checking my phone" he said.

The food was delicious, but I felt distant from Cooper.

Sometimes I feel as if I don't know him. He seems like a total stranger. Like today. I know he is hiding something. But I am scared to ask because I don't want to bring "Josephine's" name. I am scared to know if he is still talking to her. I didn't want to know, but somewhere my inner voice told me, "he is talking to her again."

We finished lunch, and Cooper dropped me home.

He was in a hurry. I don't know why.

He didn't talk much, he didn't laugh much, and he looked occupied with something else.

I saw his car going until it faded away, and I came to my flat.

I couldn't sleep that night.

I texted Cooper, "Are you talking to her again? You were busy tonight."

"No, I am not talking." He replied.

I was just busy with work-related things.

"Okay, good night" I said.

"Goodnight," he said.

I looked at my phone for a few minutes to see his message again, which says I love you, but he didn't message me.

I started becoming anxious day by day and depressed. Even a little bit of ignorance by Cooper made me depressed and stressed. I couldn't sleep the whole night thinking that what's going on with him? Why was he on his phone most of the time?

I took a sleeping pill around 5 a.m. and slept.

I missed my class again as I woke up the next day around 11. A little bit of change in Cooper affects me so much. I don't want to go to college. I don't want to talk to anybody. I don't want to get up. He has this weird effect on me. What I feel for him is more than love.

I was never stressed, anxious, or depressed before in my life, but now a small change in my life makes me feel everything. I cannot sleep without sleeping pills, I cannot eat, and I cannot smile.

I checked my phone and read Cooper's message.

"My mom is visiting me tomorrow. She will stay with me."

"That's great! Have a good time with her" I replied.

"You have to meet her" he sent the message again.

"I will try" I replied back.

Why would he want me to meet his mom if he is not serious about me? Or he is serious about me. That's why he wants me to meet his mom. I rubbed my face in confusion. "aaaarrghhhh—fuck you, Cooper"—I screamed.

I was feeling very low. I called my sister and talked for 25 minutes. I told her to come and visit me. I felt like I would be fine if I spent some time with her. Nobody in my family knows about Cooper. I never got that assurance from him. I love him more than he loves me, so I never told anybody about him, not even Leila. And the recent incidents confused me a lot.

Out of everything, Cooper cheating on me and choosing someone else over me scares me the most.

I called Leila to come over or take me out. She said she would pick me up in an hour, and we would go out for a nice coffee.

I met Leila in the parking lot, and she decided to go to Cooper's café. I told her to change the venue, but she insisted that she wanted to have coffee at the same café.

I didn't want to face Cooper. I prayed that he wouldn't come there tonight.

When we reached the café, I saw Josephine on the stairs, and she looked back at me. I never got positive vibes from her. Her eyes feel weird. Her persona was weird. As if she has a problem with me. Her face when she looks at me makes me feel like she hates me for being with Cooper.

I didn't see Cooper.

Leila and I ordered coffee and talked about our usual university stuff. Leila was worried about me and why I was not attending classes.

"Why are you not coming to university?" she asked me.

"I don't know. I just don't feel like coming" I said.

"Are you okay? You sound low" she asked.

"I am fine. Don't worry" I said.

I asked her about her classes and about her friends so that she could focus on herself and not ask about me.

She told me that she has gotten a scholarship offer for a masters from the university and how happy she is. She looked happy and content.

I kept listening to her, nodding my neck with a 'yes' and agreeing with everything she was saying.

My phone rang, and it was Cooper's message.

"Where are you? What are you doing?"

"Here in your café with Leila" I replied.

"Why didn't you tell me that you were coming?" He replied.

"I thought you must be busy" I answered.

"Josephine is here. Didn't she tell you that I am here" I messaged again.

"I don't talk to her" he replied.

Again, my inner voice told me that Josephine must have told him that I am here. Otherwise, why would he ask me all of a sudden, "Where am I?"

I looked up on my left and saw Josephine busy typing on her phone.

My hearing skipped a beat, and I thought she must be talking to Cooper.

I don't know what to do with my thoughts. Why can't I stop thinking about it? If Cooper had told me that he was not talking to her, then I should trust him.

I took a deep breath and comforted myself with my words.

Chapter-14

I got up next morning at 8 a.m. to go to the university. At 8.30, Cooper messaged me.

"Hey, mom is here. Come home, and we will all go shopping."

I didn't tell him that I had a class.

I said, "okay."

One thing I didn't like about Cooper was that he always acted as if nothing had happened. He forgot so easily that earlier his ex called late at night, and now Josephine. He wants me to act normal as well. I acted normally, but my heart is still heavy because somewhere in it I knew something was wrong. Something was there that I didn't know about. But as soon as I see Cooper, everything goes away.

His few words of comfort and love make me feel better.

"I missed my class again" I told myself.

I have missed a lot, and I don't know how I am going to cover it up. But nothing is more important to me than Cooper. I wish he would know one day that he means the world to me. I took out my floral maxi dress and got ready with a little makeup. I don't know how his mom is, what he told her about me, or how she is going to react when she meets me. Will she like me or not?

I booked the cab and went to Cooper's house. I took a few deep breaths before knocking at his door.

He opened the gate. I went inside. His mom was right there in the kitchen, and she came out when she saw me.

"Hello, dear. How are you?" she asked and hugged me.

"I am fine, thank you"—I hugged her back.

Cooper looked at my face and winked at me. I smiled and went inside his lounge on the sofa.

"I love your dress. You look wonderful" his mom said.

"Thanks, Aunty" I told her.

"So, what do you do?" she asked.

"She wants to become a writer" Cooper replied without waiting for me to answer.

"Yes, someday hopefully" I said.

"Do you want tea?" she asked.

"Yes, sure" I said.

She got up and went straight into the kitchen, and Cooper followed her.

"I like her. She is so nice" I heard his mom telling Cooper.

"She is just a friend," Cooper said.

Something inside me shattered, but I smiled when I saw them both with a tray in one hand and plates of cookies in the other. We finished our tea. His mom went inside to change, and me and Cooper waited for her to come back.

Cooper got up and kissed me, and I kissed him back.

"I love you," he said.

"I love you too," I said back.

We left for parking as soon as his mom came.

His mom sat with him in front, and I took my seat in the back. I read my book and saw Cooper looking at me a few times from the rear-view mirror.

His mom asked me about my family, my siblings, what they do, and what my plans are for the future.

I like his mother. A sweet and loving lady.

I saw Cooper's hand beside his driving seat, asking for my hand to hold. I gave my hand to him. He held it while driving with one hand. He held it until his mother turned towards me and asked, "Do you live far from here?"

I took off my hand from his and told her, "No, not that much. It's 20 minutes away from Cooper's house."

Cooper smiled from the rear-view mirror as he noticed I was nervous when his mother looked at me while holding his hand.

I smiled back.

We reached the parking lot of the mall. Cooper's mom decided to buy a purse rather than a few dresses.

We went to the store, and she asked me to help her choose.

Cooper touched my back and hands every now and then when he noticed his mom was busy shopping. I like it when he does that.

I checked my phone. "I love you" he messaged.

"I love you too," I replied.

I looked at him. He was standing near his mom. He smiled at me, and I smiled at him.

We had lunch after the shopping, and I told Cooper to drop me home before going back to his home.

I asked his mom to come upstairs, but she said she was tired and would rest for some time.

Cooper messaged me, "Can I come to your place late at night?"

"Sure, come over" I replied.

I took a shower and asked Mary to make tea for me.

"Madam, we are running out of groceries" Mary said.

"Let's go now. I am free" I said.

I went to the nearest grocery store to my flat. It had everything, from vegetables to fresh chicken.

I bought my favorite kimchi ramen, a few cereals, and chocolates, while Mary filled the basket with rice, flour, fruits, detergent, vegetables, meat, and tissue rolls.

I kept thinking about Cooper. He doesn't leave my mind for a second. I paid money at the counter, and Cooper was there in the back of my mind.

I walked back home, and I kept thinking about him. It's been a year, and not even a single day, hour, minute, or second has passed since I didn't think about him.

Sometimes I wonder if he thinks about me like I do.

Sometimes I think we are not on the same page. I give more than I get back. I am the weaker one in this relationship. I am more vulnerable, while Cooper is strong and doesn't give a damn about me.

I ordered a chocolate cake for Cooper because I know he loves to eat dessert. He has a sweet tooth.

Cooper rang the bell around 11.30 p.m. I took a deep breath, fixed my hair, and opened the door.

There he was, smiling attractively in a green shirt and blue jeans.

We hugged each other, and he came inside.

I pinched his nose. "You look so cute" I said.

"Not more than you" he said.

Cooper never complimented me much. I think a bit of complimenting, which he does sometimes, is something he has learned from me.

I love to sit with him alone. Just me and Cooper. It means much more to me than any expensive restaurant.

I and Cooper, Cooper and I.

I love it when he is available exclusively for me. I prefer to sit with him at home rather than go out with him.

The second place that I love after home is his car. Because he holds my hand, and we are together without any disturbance.

I went inside the kitchen to bring water for him. He came inside and stood so close to me that I felt his chest touching my back. He hugged me from behind while I poured water from the bottle into the glass.

I turned my face toward him and gave him the glass. He took one sip and kissed me.

I felt his cold lips on mine. I kissed him back. He kissed my neck, and I felt my heart drop as he rubbed his cold lips over my neck.

He slowly took his hand down on my trouser, and I hugged him tightly.

He put the glass down on the slab, dipped his finger in cold water, then took inside my trouser and pushed his finger inside.

"Oh, Cooper"—I screamed in his ear.

Those cold fingers made me crazy, and I couldn't open my eyes until I finished.

"Do you like doing it in the kitchen?" he asked.

"I love it" I said while laughing.

I put my arms around his neck and kissed him.

I took the cake to the table, and we both ate it while laughing and talking to each other. I checked the phone, and it was already 1 a.m.

"What the fuck is wrong with the time when you are with me" I said, angrily looking at the time.

"Even if I sit with you the whole day, it's not enough" he said.

His phone rang suddenly.

"Lawyer calling..."

Why would a lawyer call him at midnight?

Cooper didn't pick. Lawyer called again. Cooper missed the call again.

Who is Lawyer? I asked.

"He is my mom's lawyer. Working on some legal issues on her property."

"Why is he calling you at one a.m.?" Pick up his call, I said.

"No, leave it" Cooper said nervously.

"What are you hiding, Cooper?" I asked him.

"I am not hiding anything" he said, and he went to the bathroom.

His phone rang again, but this time a number flashed on the screen.

I took a photo of the phone number on my phone and checked on WhatsApp.

What I saw on WhatsApp has blown away my mind.

I checked the picture on WhatsApp closely, and it was Josephine's photo.

I was numb.

Cooper came out. I didn't react.

"I will go now. Mom is alone" he said.

"Okay" I said quietly.

He left.

I came to my bed. I checked her WhatsApp again. It means Lawyer is Josephine.

When Cooper didn't answer her call, she called from another number. I clicked the photo of her other number and checked in on my phone.

God has been giving me signs about Cooper, but I didn't want to accept them.

I took a screenshot of her number and display picture and sent it to Cooper.

"So, this is your lawyer" I sent a message.

"It's not what you are thinking" he replied.

"I can't believe you are talking to her again. You promised me that you would never talk to her again" I replied.

"Her husband is a lawyer, and I talked to her regarding some issues" he replied.

"For fuck's sake, you found her husband only to resolve your problem with? I am sure she will not talk about you to her husband" I replied.

"Go to hell, Cooper, you have made me insane" I sent the message and switched off my phone.

After half an hour, the doorbell rang again. I opened the door, and it was Cooper standing.

I came inside without saying anything. He followed me.

"Why did you switch off your phone?" he asked.

"What do you want me to do? Listen to your lies again" I said.

I didn't lie to you. I talked to her because of my mom, he said.

"Oh, don't give me this bullshit, Cooper" I said angrily.

"Why can't you stay without talking to that woman?" I asked.

You don't feel what I feel because I never made you go through things that you made me go through. Even I do something like this. Maybe you won't even care because you don't love me. You are bored of me. You want a new person in your life. You are emotionally unavailable, Cooper. You need someone all the time to make you feel better about yourself. Maybe you have some hidden childhood trauma.

"Am I not enough for you?" I asked.

"You are enough for me, Serah", he said softly.

"Then why are you doing all this with me. Why can't you let me stay in peace?"

"I am happy with you" I told Cooper, and tears started rolling down my cheeks.

He came closer to me and hugged me.

"I am sorry" he said.

I cried and cried.

"Please don't cry" he said, and he hugged me tighter.

"Go home, Cooper. I am fine" I told him.

He left.

My whole body was shivering. I don't know if he is cheating on me or if he is actually talking about work. But one thing I am sure about is that 'Josephine' likes Cooper and hates me. I suddenly remember her eyes staring at me, then looking at Cooper every minute.

"I hope you die, Josephine" I screamed.

I couldn't sleep again that night. I feel I am depressed. I took sleeping pills and slept again.

The next morning, I woke up at 12 p.m. but stayed in bed the whole day.

"Madam, should I get you something to eat?" Mary asked me with concern.

"I don't want to eat, and don't come into my room again. I am sleeping" I said.

"Okay madam" Mary closed the door and left.

I picked up my phone and saw a few missed calls from Cooper and two messages. I didn't open the message and didn't call him back.

I am going crazy. Why is my mind occupied with him? I was so angry that I hit the wall with my hand.

I want to run away from Cooper and never see his face. But I can't live without him.

My mother called me.

"I want to come home for a few days" I told her.

"Oh, honey, you are always welcome" she said.

I decided to go home, see a therapist, and not think about Cooper.

I messaged Cooper that I was going home after two days for a few weeks.

"What? Why?" he replied.

"I am not feeling fine mentally." I replied back.

"Meet me tonight. Let's go to the bar" he messaged.

"Pick me up" I replied.

"Okay. Be ready by 10 p.m."

I put down my phone, put my head down on my legs, and hugged my legs. I closed my eyes and thought about the good times with Cooper. I thought about recent times as well.

I was going crazy. Cooper doesn't love me anymore. There is a change in his behavior.

Is he seeing Josephine? I cried so much that I started screaming in pain.

"Madam, are you okay?" Mary ran to my room.

"I am fine. Please switch off the lights" I said.

I took anti-stress pills and closed my eyes.

Is being in love so painful? Does it make your life hell when someone you love doesn't love you back? Does love make you numb? Oh, Cooper, what have you done to me? Have you ever loved me for a minute, or was I just a time pass for you? You already have too many backup options in case I ever leave. You will not care about me.

I woke up after an hour, washed my face, and put on my normal tee and trousers.

Cooper came to pick me up, and we both went to the bar he chose for us.

"Why are you going?" he asked.

"You have Josephine here. Don't worry about me" I said.

He smiled.

How the fuck can he smile? Does it even matter to him how much I hate it when he takes my feelings so lightly? Does he even have a heart? Why is he so cruel?

"Yes, laugh. Be happy with her when I am gone" I said.

"I don't need anyone. I have you" he replied.

We reached the bar. He held my hand while I went inside. I let him.

I ordered Coke, and he ordered beer.

I saw a girl looking at Cooper, and Cooper was staring at her.

"Stop looking at her. What do you want from her?" I asked.

"Nothing" he said, and he laughed again.

The woman came to Cooper and gave him a bottle of beer.

"Thank you," Cooper said.

"What's your name?" she asked.

"I am Cooper, and you?" he replied with enthusiasm.

"I am Maya" she replied with a smile on her face.

She gave him another bottle of beer, and he drank it while talking to her.

He made me feel like he doesn't know me at all. He kept talking to her, and I sat alone.

She opened another bottle and passed it to him.

"Would you like to dance with me?" Maya asked.

"Why not?" Cooper replied.

Cooper and Maya went together and danced. I felt my tears rolling down my cheeks while looking at both of them dancing.

She kept touching Cooper, and Cooper half hugged her while dancing.

I couldn't stop my tears, so I recorded a video.

"Hey, your friend made our video" Maya said to Cooper.

Cooper came to me and asked me to delete.

I deleted the video, and he went back to her for a dance.

Millions of thoughts came to my mind as I watched Cooper dancing with Maya.

What does Cooper want from me? How can he do that in front of my eyes? I kept crying. He noticed me crying but ignored me and kept dancing. He was drunk.

He drank 12 bottles of beer with Maya.

I looked at both of them and wondered, " My existence is nothing for him. My tears are nothing to him. I am just someone he needs when he is alone. I am just a toy with whom he likes to enjoy and play.

I remembered all those times when Cooper ignored me and flirted with different girls at different times. And all along, I knew that the love I have for Cooper would ruin me one day, and I also knew that I would let it. I love hard, and people at this age don't understand.

Cooper felt uneasy, and he moved out of the bar. I followed him. He puked everything he drank and was almost dead because of the 12 bottles. I cleaned his mouth with the sleeve of my t-shirt. I held him, took him to the cab, and dropped him home. I went home. My mind was numb. I couldn't believe what I saw.

I blocked his number, took a few sleeping pills, and slept.

The next morning, I woke with a thud on the door.

"Madam, your friend is here" Mary said.

"I woke up, freshened myself up, and went to the lounge area.

"Hey" I said.

"Why did you block me?" he asked angrily.

"I don't want to talk to you anymore, Cooper" I said.

"Why, what did I do?" he asked.

I laughed surprisingly. "Really?"

Go dance with Maya. Hug her, kiss her. I said with utter jealously.

"And what will you do? Make my video instead of stopping me?" he replied.

"I made the video so that I could show you what you did when you were sober, but you made me delete it" I said.

"If you had loved me, you would have stopped me" he said.

"Oh my god, I can't believe what you are saying. Are you a kid? Don't you know what you are doing?" I said.

"I didn't do anything" he said and left.

Instead of being sorry or feeling guilty, he blamed me for not stopping him. I was shocked to see that, for once, he didn't even apologize.

I packed my bags and left for the train station, as I didn't want to stay here anymore.

Chapter-15

I didn't inform Cooper. I didn't want to talk to him anymore. I didn't want him to know my whereabouts.

I reached home, and my mom and dad welcomed me with my favorite foods and drinks. I was not happy, and it was clearly visible on my face. I couldn't smile, and I couldn't eat. I was highly anxious and deeply stressed. My mental health was ruined. Suddenly, Cooper seemed so strange that it was very hard for me to digest that I spent my days and nights with him.

I didn't message or call Cooper the whole day, and neither did he.

I waited for him to tell me that he was sorry and that he still loves me. I wanted him to give me assurance which I always craved in this relationship but never got.

I went to my room, and went through my old stuff. My books, my clothes, and my cupboard when I heard a message beep on my phone. I prayed that it was Cooper.

"Cooper is having coffee and a nice chit-chat with Josephine" - the text said with a picture of Cooper's café, with Cooper and Josephine sitting on different seats but both using the phone as if talking on messages.

I saw the box of my medicine and gulped all my sleeping pills.

I collapsed in my room.

I slightly opened my eyes, and the next thing I saw was doctors around me talking to my mother and father about how unstable my mental health is and how my brain is affected by abnormalities. I heard my mother crying and talking to the doctors, saying that she doesn't have any idea what's going on with me or why I attempted suicide. Then I closed my eyes, and those three years flashed in front of my eyes I spent with him, how I loved him, forgave him, and loved him again while being manipulated by him. He continued to do things in parallel without considering my feelings.

I woke up after 18 hours and saw my mom sitting beside me with a lot of questions in her eyes, which I was not ready to answer. She hugged me and cried her eyes out without questioning the situation.

"I am fine, Mom"- I said to her.

She gave me a few slices of apple to eat. I finished eating and closed my eyes again.

My heart is still full of him. After going through the mess, he has no idea about, I still feel either Cooper or nobody else, and the truth is, I love him, but he is not in love with me, and until I stop loving him, no one else stands a chance. I will leave such an imprint on his heart that anyone he entertains after me will have to know me in order to understand him.

I thought about the message I got, and a lot of questions came into my mind.

Does he sleep peacefully at night? Does he not think about me, where I am, or what I am doing? Does he never think about how he broke my heart? Does he never think about me for a few minutes before sleeping? Does he never miss me?

Is he never thinking about the time or the moments we shared together? Is he never thinking about the time we spent making love, kissing each other, holding hands, and cuddling?

I usually don't wish the worst on anyone, and I still don't. I hope you feel how you made me feel and never repeat it for anyone else who decides to love you. Looking out of the window of the psychiatric ward, I murmured while tears rolled down my cheeks, and my chest felt heavy in pain and I felt a lump in my throat. I screamed my lungs out. A few nurses ran towards me and took me to my bed, where I was given an injection. I closed my eyes while still feeling the same pain in my chest and tears flowing from my eyes.

To be continued...

www.ingramcontent.com/pod-product-compliance
Lightning Source LLC
LaVergne TN
LVHW041608070526
838199LV00052B/3031